They Say
Sarah

They Say Sarah

Pauline
Delabroy-Allard

Translated from the French by
Adriana Hunter

Other Press
New York

Originally published in France as *Ça raconte Sarah*
by Les Éditions de Minuit, Paris, in 2018.
First published in English as *All About Sarah*
by Harvill Secker, London, in 2020.

Excerpts from *The Years* by Annie Ernaux, translated by Alison L Strayer,
published by Fitzcarraldo Editions; "The Lilacs" by Louis Aragon, in its
original French: "O claire nuit jour obscur / Mon absente entre mes bras /
Et rien d'autre en moi ne dure / Que ce que tu murmuras," published in
Le Fou d'Elsa, copyright © Éditions Gallimard, Paris, 1963, translated here
by Adriana Hunter; "India Song," performed by Jeanne Moreau, music by
Carlos D'Alessio, lyrics by Marguerite Duras, translated here by Adriana
Hunter; "Mon manège à moi," performed by Edith Piaf, music by Norbert
Glanzberg, lyrics by Jean Constantin, translated here by Adriana Hunter;
"Hit the Road Jack," performed by Ray Charles, music and lyrics by
Percy Mayfield; *Death and the Maiden*, String Quartet No. 14 in D minor,
composed by Franz Schubert, words from a poem by Matthias Claudius,
translated by Richard Wigmore

Production editor: Yvonne E. Cárdenas
This book was set in 11.5/17 pt Bembo.

10 9 8 7 6 5 4 3 2 1

Library of Congress Cataloging-in-Publication Data

Names: Delabroy-Allard, Pauline, 1988- author. | Hunter, Adriana, translator.
Title: They say Sarah / Pauline Delabroy-Allard ; translated from the
French by Adriana Hunter.
Other titles: Ça raconte Sarah. English
Description: London : Harvill Secker, 2020.
Identifiers: LCCN 2019055972 (print) | LCCN 2019055973 (ebook) |
ISBN 9781635429855 (paperback) | ISBN 9781635429862 (ebook)
Classification: LCC PQ2704.E34433 C313 2020 (print) |
LCC PQ2704.E34433 (ebook) | DDC 843/.92—dc23
LC record available at https://lccn.loc.gov/2019055972
LC ebook record available at https://lccn.loc.gov/2019055973

Publisher's Note
This is a work of fiction. Names, characters, places, and incidents either
are the product of the author's imagination or are used fictitiously, and any
resemblance to actual persons, living or dead, events, or locales is entirely
coincidental.

All there will be is silence and no words to say it.

Annie Ernaux, *The Years*

Oh clear night day of dark mists
My absent love in my arms here
No other part of me persists
But what you whispered in my ear

Louis Aragon, "The Lilacs"

In the half-light of three a.m., I wake. The heat is killing me but I daren't get up to open the window a little wider. I'm lying in her bed in this room I know so well, next to her body, which is asleep at last after a long battle with the fears that eat away at everything, her head, her stomach, her heart. We talked a lot to dispel them, to drive them back to the frontiers of the night, we made love and I stroked her body to soothe it. I ran my hand over her shoulders, then down her arms, I snuggled against her back and fondled the soft flesh of her back-side for a long time. I listened to her breathing, waiting for her short inhalations to become lighter, for the sobs to grow further apart, for peace to find a way in at last.

It's so hot in this room. I want to move around a bit, feel the air on my face. But her body's in contact with mine, her hand resting on my arm, and moving would risk toppling the edifice I spent so long constructing. Her sleep is like a sandcastle. One move and it'll come crashing down. One move and her eyes will snap open. One move and it will have to start all over again. I listen to the purr of her sleep-laden breathing, it makes me feel like laughing with pleasure, with high spirits finally — momentarily — regained. I wish I could put the night on pause and listen to this murmuring for hours and hours, days and days, because murmuring means *I live*, it means *I exist*, it means *I'm here*. And I'm here too, right next to her.

My sweltering body stays perfectly still. If not disturbing the sandcastle of her sleep means dying of the heat, well, then I'm happy to die of the heat. Outside in the grayish dark that I can see through the window, birds are singing. It sounds like a thousand of them vying to out-chirp each other, carving through the air in every direction like the most skilled of pilots. This crushingly hot night is their own private Bastille Day, they're performing aerial acrobatics to their hearts' content, inventing increasingly perilous feats. In the trees in the distance, suburban turtledoves greet the very first glimpses of dawn with their penetrating calls. I watch their shadows dart across the dirty sky. The heat's killing me. I wait.

I turn to look at her body as it lies, unmoving, on its back, perfectly naked. I study the delicacy of her ankles, the jut of her hip bones, her supple stomach and the slender shape of her arms, the swell of her lips, bearing the lightest of smiles. I consider the damage caused by the illness on this body I love so dearly, the tiny black dots where her stomach has been injected again and again, the scar near her armpit, the hole under her collarbone. I look at her restful face, perfectly restful, her chin proud even in sleep, her downy cheeks, the surprising, abrupt line of her nose, her mauve eyelids closed at last. I look at her completely bald head. In the half-light of three a.m., I watch her sleep.

Here in the clammy darkness I can't take my eyes off her naked body and waxy scalp. Her deathly profile.

I

1

It's all about Sarah, her unique brand of beauty, her sharp, rare bird's beak of a nose, the unusual color of her eyes, stone-like, green, but not really, not green, her absinthe, malachite, faded gray-green eyes, her snake eyes with their drooping lids. It's all about the spring when she came into my life as if stepping onto a stage, with gusto, triumphant. Victorious.

2

It's a spring like any other, a spring to depress the best of us. There are magnolias in bloom in squares all over Paris, and I have this idea that they chafe the hearts of people who notice them. They certainly chafe my heart, those magnolia flowers in the squares. I look at them every evening on my way home from the school and, every evening, their large pale petals sting my eyes slightly. It's a spring like any other, with impromptu showers, the smell of wet tarmac, a sort of lightness in the air, a breath of happiness that sings softly about the fragility of it all.

This particular spring I walk around like a ghost. I'm living a life I never thought I'd live, a life alone with a child whose father vanished without any warning. One day, or rather one evening, he left the apartment and then. And then nothing. So this is possible: overnight, and I mean literally overnight, between two people who've loved each other for years, there can suddenly be no eye contact, no words, no conversation, no ranting, no anger, no understanding, no tenderness, no love. This lunacy, this aberration is what constitutes me from one day to the next. I think life will stop right here. I don't hope for anything or anyone. There's a new boy in my life, a Bulgarian boy. When I mention him I say my partner. He's my partner in crime, yes, that's it, he's my partner in the crime of this desolate life. I'm waiting. There's a word going round and round obsessively in my head, the word *latency*. I keep thinking I must look it up in the dictionary. I know I'm experiencing a period of latency. I don't know how long it will go on, and what event will bring it to an end. In the meantime every day is much the same, what with my responsibilities as a young mother, my responsibilities as a young teacher, my responsibilities as a daughter, a friend and the girlfriend of the Bulgarian boy. I'm making a point of living life. Not really living it. But

I'm a good girl. I stick out my tongue with concentration. I'm well dressed, polite and charming. I bicycle around the streets of the Fifteenth Arrondissement with my child in a seat behind me. We go to museums, to the cinema, to the botanical gardens. I think I'm pretty, people say I'm kind and attentive to others. I don't make any waves. I'm mother to a perfect child, teacher to remarkable students, daughter to wonderful parents. Life could have gone on like this for ages. A long tunnel with no surprises and no mystery to it.

3

A shrill blast of the doorbell, like a whip crack, in the middle of this apartment with its endemic starchy atmosphere. We're done up to the nines for New Year's Eve, three couples eyeing each other surreptitiously, surprised to be here and terribly overdressed. It's all so forced, the way the apartment is decorated, the topics of conversation, the guests' outfits. All so studied. Serious. Rigid. The doorbell seems to make the furniture jump – it's obviously not used to the intrusion. Mutterings. Oh, it's Sarah, someone says delightedly. I don't know who Sarah is. Yes you do, I'm told, you've already met. I'm told when and where. No recollection whatsoever. The lady of the house goes to open the door. Yes, it's Sarah. I don't recognize her.

She's late, out of breath, laughing. An unexpected tornado. She talks loudly, fast, hauling from her bag a bottle of wine, things to eat, a profusion of stuff. She takes off her scarf, her coat, her gloves and hat. She dumps everything on the floor, on the cream carpeting. She apologizes, jokes, turns circles. She talks all wrong, using coarse words that seem to hang in the air long after they've been spoken. She makes too much noise. There was nothing, silence, the occasional affected laugh, punctilious facial expressions, and all at once she's the only thing here. It's annoying. The lady of the house frowns, in her evening dress. Sarah doesn't notice, and energetically kisses everyone hello. She leans toward me, she smells of crisp late-December air. She has the rosy cheeks of someone who's hurried. She's wearing far too much makeup. She's not very well dressed, she isn't wearing her best outfit, she's not elegant, she hasn't put her hair in a sophisticated updo. She talks a lot, jumps at a glass of wine that's handed to her, roars with laughter at a quip. She's animated, enthused, impassioned.

It's like a slow-motion sequence. The glass slips from my hand, my partner gasps Oh no!, the glass spins through the air, everyone watches, no one can do a thing, it's already too late, the glass crashes without a sound onto the cream carpet, its entire contents spilling and creating an abstract shape, red wine on the cream carpet, a beautiful minimalist painting, I go white and then red with embarrassment, the lady of the house bridles, in her evening dress, it's a catastrophe, a disaster, this red form on the cream carpet, something unforeseen, an accident. A breach.

Later we sit down for dinner. We go into ecstasies over the gorgeous tablecloth, the gorgeous place settings, the gorgeous menu. There's a seating plan. There are seven of us. The lady of the house announces who's sitting where, in her evening dress. Sarah is seated next to me. On my right.

4

She's a violinist. She smokes cigarettes. She's wearing too much makeup, it's even worse up close. She talks loudly, laughs a lot, is funny in her own way. She uses words I don't know. She has her own personal slang. She plays with language, inventing expressions, making rhymes for the fun of it. She talks about amusing things, stories full of twists and turns. She complies good-naturedly with my requests for more details. She's alive. Over the course of the conversation, I find out that she really likes board games, hiking up mountains and singing with the people she loves. She's been having therapy for several years now. She lies down on the couch. She thinks it strange, talking about oneself in frosty silence.

But she keeps going back, she thinks it's important. Twice a week. Sometimes three times.

5

When we leave the building in the early hours we all walk to the nearest Métro station together. Farewell hugs on the pavement, with that peculiar feeling of being in the first day of a new year. We're already talking about the spilled glass of wine as a memorable anecdote, going over the scene, adding details, describing the lady of the house and her frown, and her evening dress.

My partner, referring to Sarah: "And what about her? What a weird girl!"

6

She writes to me over the next few days, the first days of the new year. It's January but yet again the miracle happens. Yet again winter admits defeat, drags its heels a little longer and tries one final flourish, but it's too late, it's over, the spring has won. When I emerge from the school building, the sky seems to go on for ever, blueish, a slightly washed-out blue, like dyed fabric. Nonchalant clouds scud on the wind. The moon, a discreet presence in a corner, is there too, and the fact that day and night rub shoulders amicably makes me shiver a little. Shadows grow shorter by the day on the tarmac, and I walk home in a gilded glow like no other light. The streets of lime-stone houses are full of birdsong, uninterrupted chattering, and you can almost hear the buds appearing on branches, green, delicate, fragile. I look at the light tingeing the tops of buildings pink. How many more times will I be granted the huge privilege of witnessing all this? How many more times will I be able to watch this perfor-mance? Once? Fifteen times? Sixty-three? Is this the last time, I wonder, is this the last time I'll feel the quivering of a new season in my body? She writes to me in the first days of the new year. A few words, at first, to which I reply politely. Then more and more. She says it would be good to meet up. She suggests going to a concert at the Philharmonic Society. She suggests going to the cinema, the theater. We meet once, twice, more and more. The winter gradually creeps away, without a sound.

7

One March morning she emails to say she's in the neigh-borhood of the school where I work and asks if we can have lunch together. I can't. I don't have time, I have too much to do, it would be awkward if my colleagues noticed. I say yes. I make my escape at the appointed hour, a pecu-liar happiness in my heart. It's a beautiful day. She's waiting for me at the Métro station. She starts talking straight away, very quickly, very loudly, gesticulating a lot. Her eyes shine. She walks in the street, apparently fantastically indifferent to the cars that could knock her down. I expect she doesn't notice that I want to pull her back by her sleeve every five minutes because she seems so preoccupied, and I'm frightened there'll be an accident. She's alive.

8

In the Korean restaurant she talks so much that the waiter comes to take our order at least three times. She's never ready. She says she can't choose, it's a problem, in life. She wants everything and nothing. She tells me how during the strikes that crippled France in 1995 she learned to hitchhike around Paris. She was fifteen that year. I gaze at her and I've already stopped listening to her, I watch her and wonder what she looked like, at fifteen, and what it must have been like, life then. Paris completely paralyzed, rendered mute without all those cars to buzz through the streets, or at least a little quieter, hoarse. Paris with a frog in its throat. And a fifteen-year-old Sarah in the middle of it all, probably with drooping eyelids already, probably with her violin case on her back already, teetering like a tightrope-walker along the edges of pavements in the Sixteenth Arrondissement, where she grew up, her thumb out, in the hope that someone would take her on her way. To school, to the conservatory, to her friends for music practice. To the ends of the earth. That's what I imagine. At fifteen, Sarah hitchhiked through a voiceless Paris because she wanted to be taken to the ends of the earth. That's what I imagine and that's what I hold on to.

Later, when she walks back to the school with me, or maybe it's during the same conversation, she describes the first time she drank beer with her father. It wasn't very late in the day. I think I've got this right: as she recalls it, her father had come to pick her up when she'd been away somewhere for a week, or was taking her somewhere to catch a train. Anyway, there was a station involved. That's how I see the scene in my mind's eye. Sarah and her father together, sitting on the metal chairs of a station café. It's daytime, broad daylight, that I do remember her mentioning when she told me about this memory. She's a young woman, I picture her beautiful but I really have no idea. As for him, it's difficult to say what he looked like. Fifteen years ago would he have had dark hair? Been full of smiles? And jokes, as he sat facing his teenage daughter? The apple of his eye, the light of his life, his little darling. She laughs as she describes the scene, I don't know why but she laughs, in hindsight, years later, laughs uproariously about the look on his face when she ordered her first half, about the pride she felt, the assurance it gave her. I imagine her swagger, the unforgettable color of the first beer ordered so boldly, in broad daylight, sitting at a café, with her father. She describes the memory and laughs, she can't stop laughing, so much so that it's almost contagious. Nearly twenty years later, she laughs as she describes her nerve.

9

I ask her how she would define *latency*. She leans in slightly as I explain that this word is superimposed onto every image of my life, I can't get it out of my head, I don't really know why but I'm obsessed with it.

After a silence: "It's the time between two major events."

10

Days go by. Spring settles in, calmly, in no hurry. It's a spring like any other, a spring to depress the best of us. Sarah settles in, settles into my life, calmly, in no rush. She invites me to the theater, the cinema. She smokes in my kitchen one evening when I ask her over for supper. She tells me a secret. She tells me she's never told this secret to anyone. She doesn't notice the turmoil I'm in. She gives me her string quartet's latest album. A Beethoven collection. She doesn't know that over the next few days I listen to it on loop. She doesn't know that I read books about chamber music. She doesn't know that I want to know everything, understand everything, be familiar with everything. She doesn't suspect for a moment that I'm furious with myself for not being a better student when I was at the conservatory.

My partner's amused by this sudden, instant, almost abrupt friendship. I don't tell him that when I have the choice between spending time with him or with her, I choose her. He and I go together to watch her play at the string-quartet biennale at the Philharmonic Society. It's on a Sunday afternoon. When we get there the auditorium is full, there are no seats left. I put up a fight with the man at the box office, make big eyes, beg and rage. My partner says it doesn't really matter, we can listen to them another time. He says for goodness' sake, come on, let's have a coffee outside, in the sunshine. I refuse to give up. I cry with anger. He doesn't understand what's happening to me. I end up getting two tickets at the last minute. We have to sit on fold-down seats, a very long way from the stage. I screw up my eyes to see what's going on. I can see the other three members of the quartet. When the four of them come onstage in single file, I'm so nervous I feel like laughing out loud. For the first time I see her with her hair done, looking elegant, distinguished. She's wearing a disconcerting concert gown, very long, black, backless. They bow to the audience before they start playing. I can't breathe. I almost clap after the first movement of the opening quartet. I don't know the form. I don't understand a thing. My eyes are pinned on her tiny figure, so far away, on the stage. The piece they play for the encore blows my mind. Someone tells me it's a movement from a Bartók quartet, all in *pizzicato*. I don't understand a word of what they're saying. I clap wildly, very loudly and for a very long time, until my palms hurt.

11

She asks me what I do with my Wednesdays when I don't have my daughter. I go to the cinema, alone. I write to let her know. I give her the name of the cinema, what time the film is on. I catch myself hoping she'll be there at the end, waiting for me. The film is about casual affairs that make it easier to forget a great love. It's in black and white. The heroine's very beautiful. It reminds me of a New Wave film. I savor this time, alone, in a cinema. I wonder whether she'll come. The film ends. I race outside. No one. It's raining. I walk briskly, with my head down, watching my ankle boots stride out all on their own over the wet cobblestones of the rue de la Verrerie. My phone rings. It's her. She asks where are you, and says I'm on rue de la Verrerie, I'm coming.

12

She tells me she's thinking of me when, on a dazzling first day of sunshine, I go to the law courts. Later, over a glass of wine, she asks me how it went. She doesn't take her eyes off me as I tell her about the waiting, the judge, my daughter's father, the decision that he'll have her every other weekend, the sun that made me far too hot, what with me being dressed all in black, in mourning for this lost love.

13

She invites me to watch a play with her at one of the Cartoucherie theaters. She waits for me at Château de Vincennes Métro station, on Line 1. She's wearing a dress that doesn't suit her at all, as usual. She greets me with a raucous laugh and talks the whole time we're walking through the Bois de Vincennes park. It's getting dark. She talks, and talks, a complete motormouth. She's alive. She asks me about my work, about the high school where I teach. She stops talking only when the lights go down. Our knees touch in the dark.

14

The theater is called Théâtre de la Tempête. That's it: tempestuous.

15

She was blown away by the play. She wants to go and congratulate the actor in the lead role. I watch her approach him, impressed by her easy confidence. She talks to him with impetuous enthusiasm. He smiles. She asks me if I'm tired or if we have time for a drink. She adds that okay so Château de Vincennes Métro station isn't the best place in the world for drinks. But there is that one bar, Les Officiers. She goes in. She sits down. She asks what draft beers they have. I say the same, exactly the same, when the waiter asks what I'd like. She looks sad, a bit deflated, I've never seen her like this. She asks if we can go out for a cigarette. She looks at her feet. It's quite chilly, in the dark night. She blows her smoke up at the sky, making a cloud to join the clouds. She looks me right in the eye. She says I think I'm in love with you.

16

She makes the beginnings of a gesture, a backward step, like a dance move, almost smiling as I stammer oh right, but, I didn't realize. She says she's going to smoke another cigarette, to celebrate this, her daring, her courage, the match flares in the darkness, the smell of sulfur will always and for ever be the smell of that admission and the relief of it, the smell of an unsayable reality finally said, the smell of the truth laid bare, brought ashore, laid at my feet like a gift.

Sulphur is one of the chalcogen elements. It's a multivalent non-metal, abundant, unremarkable and insoluble in water. Sulphur is best known in the form of yellow crystals and is found in many minerals, particularly in volcanic regions. When it burns it gives off a strong unpleasant odor. Sulfur is an element, not a compound. Atomic number: 16. Symbol: S.

17

It's all about Sarah, her mysterious beauty, the sharp lines of her gentle bird-of-prey nose, her pebble-like eyes, green, but no, not green, her unusual colored eyes, her snake eyes with their drooping lids. It's all about Sarah the impetuous, Sarah the passionate, Sarah the sulfurous, it's all about the exact moment when the match flares, the exact moment when that piece of wood becomes fire, when the spark lights up the darkness, when burning springs out of nowhere. The exact moment is tiny, everything turned upside down in barely a second. It's all about Sarah, symbol: S.

18

Sulfur. From the Latin *sulfur,* sulfur, the thunderbolt, fire from the sky. *Suffer.* First person singular. I suffer. From the Latin *suffero*, to bear, cope with, endure. Particularly in the sense of being chastised by someone, punished for something. Being subjected to a sentence.

<h1 style="text-align:center">19</h1>

She offers me this admission, like a gift. And walks off into the night. A few days later, she says yes when I suggest going to the cinema. An Alain Resnais film has just come out. It's called *Life of Riley*. She's there early. She's wearing too much makeup on her eyes, her eyes with their drooping lids. So it's March. She nods when I say it's nearly spring. She's hungry, very hungry. She asks if we can go for a bite to eat, before the film. She orders a buckwheat pancake, and buttermilk. She wants a beer after that. She orders a half of their strongest beer. The waiter asks me what I'd like. The same, exactly the same. She tells me about her last concert while we drink our beers. She describes it clearly, explains the things I don't understand. She catches my eyes hovering over her, perusing every tiny detail of her body, and her face. She asks me what I'm thinking. I dodge her questions. I don't want to answer. She doesn't give up, go on, say it, what are you thinking. I don't answer. There's that admission, like a gift, between us. My lowered eyes. It's all about that, the thundering silence and the fluffy white days you float through when you offer someone the truth.

20

More beers, after the film, the strongest they have, and for me too, the same, exactly the same. More matches struck, lighting up her snake eyes, just for a moment, before the darkness wraps around us again, on the pavement where we go out to smoke. More stubs tossed away nonchalantly. More stories told. After a while it's so late the manager tells us we must go to bed. He's closing up. It's the middle of the night, and he's tired.

Life of Riley is a French comedy-drama co-written and directed by Alain Resnais. Running time: 108 minutes. The cast includes Sabine Azéma, Hippolyte Girardot and André Dussollier. It's Resnais' last film, he died on 1 March 2014.

I don't remember anything about it.

She walks slightly ahead of me on the boulevard du Montparnasse on that March night. She doesn't seem as drunk as I am. She's alive. She doesn't see that I'm making a point of following her footsteps, that my mind's in a fog and the road surface is pitching slightly. All at once she spins round, very quickly, and puts her mouth to mine.

She hails a taxi. She strokes my thigh in the back of the cab. Her eyes shine. She climbs the two flights of stairs to my apartment behind me, so close to me I can feel her breath on my calves. She comes into my apartment. She pours herself a glass of water. She takes off her makeup, next to me, in the tiny bathroom. The mirror shows our two faces: surprised but also serious, terribly serious. She slips under the duvet, next to me, in the wavering light of the dawning day. She whispers that she's never made love with a woman. She asks and you. I say me neither, the same, exactly the same. She strokes my face, my neck, my breasts.

21

Her perfume. Her smell. Her neck. Her hair. Her hands. Her fingers. Her buttocks. Her calves. Her nails. Her earlobes. Her moles. Her thighs. Her violet vulva. Her hips. Her navel. Her nipples. Her shoulders. Her knees. Her armpits. Her cheeks. Her tongue.

The next day she leaves me on a street corner, on the way to the school. She tilts her chin at me and launches off down the pavement. She leaves me, unaware that my hands are shaking, and they don't stop shaking all day, incredulous at what they did, at what they touched. She leaves me, unaware that at the end of the morning I make an appointment with the doctor, incapable of working any longer, that he signs me off sick for two days, that I dive under my duvet in the middle of the afternoon to sleep in the smell of her. The next day I open up my sicknote to send it off. The doctor wrote: Change in general state of health.

22

Making love with a woman: tempestuous.

23

Over the next few days all I think about is what happened, images come and go the moment I close my eyes. I never thought I'd touch a woman's body, that I'd like it to distraction and would think about it constantly, day and night. She's always on my mind. She haunts me, naked, divine, a ghost that makes my veins swell, makes my snatch slick. It's a revelation, an illumination, an epiphany.

24

After the first night, being away from her is an aberration.

25

She writes to me, a lot. In the separate lives we lead, words whizz back and forth all day, and late into the night. She writes to me, I reply, she writes again. She asks me questions, do I like it too, have I been obsessed about it ever since too. My answers: yes, yes. Yes. Life around me no longer exists. Neither does the outside world. There's only her now. Her, her snake eyes, her breasts, her bum.

She disregards her schedule whenever she can, to see me. It's always the same arrangement. She comes to my place, my apartment. She whispers when I ask her not to speak so loudly because my child's asleep in the next room. She lets the exquisite pleasure of supper last that little bit longer, every time. She tells stories. She looks me right in the eye as she drinks her glass of wine. She smokes out of the window. And then she can't take it any longer, she comes over to me. She breathes my smell, breathes me in. It's all about that: the sulfurous, suffering, tempestuous breath.

She doesn't know that her smell ties my stomach in knots. She doesn't realize that nothing interests me any more, nothing and no one. She has a *pain au chocolat* in the morning, with a latte. I start having a *pain au chocolat* in the morning, with a latte. She wears mascara every day. I start wearing mascara every day. She uses crude words I don't know. I adopt them into my vocabulary. She presses her breasts against mine as soon as we're alone together, and she hugs me till I can't breathe, as if she wishes we could be just one body. She goes on tour with her quartet. She goes off to Brussels, and Budapest. She writes to me the whole time. She asks if it's hard for me too, always being separated. She begs me to wait for her, she promises to come back as soon as possible. She's captain of the ship in this tempestuous storm. I become a sailor's wife.

A happy coincidence in the calendar. The quartet is playing in Venice just when I'm going there for a holiday. I'm traveling with a girlfriend and tell her that an acquaintance of mine, Sarah, is also in Venice and it would be nice to see her. We arrange to meet on the Campo San Bartolomeo one April afternoon. On the appointed day my friend and I get lost in the labyrinthine streets of Venice. I'm worried we'll be late. I walk quickly. My heart beats furiously, my head aches weirdly, my temples hurt. I chivvy my friend, who's ambling, spellbound by the city. I haven't seen Sarah for several days. In this Italian light such a long way from my apartment in Paris, it seems almost impossible that this thing we've been living for several weeks – our mouths sealed together, our bodies cleaved against each other – can be real. It suddenly feels impossible that this thing can be going on. I even wonder if she exists, if Sarah does, or if I dreamed her up.

Campo San Bartolomeo, sometimes called Campo San Bortolo, is a small square close to the Rialto. It's very busy and very popular, and is one of the local Venetians' favorite meeting places. In the middle of the square stands a bronze statue of Carlo Goldoni, a seventeenth-century Venetian dramatist, founder of modern Italian theater and author of, amongst others,

L'incognita (*The Unknown Woman*), *La putta onorata* (*The Honourable Maiden*), *La dama prudente* (*The Prudent Lady*), *La donna stravagante* (*The Extravagant Woman*), *La donna bizarra* (*The Bizarre Woman*) and *La donna sola* (*The Lone Woman*).

There's no one on the Campo San Bartolomeo. Well, yes, hundreds of people, busy Venetians, tourists of all nationalities, groups, children, probably all very glad to be here, in Venice, on an April day. But no one. I study every face, and don't find her. I was sure of it, I invented her, I invented the whole thing, it doesn't exist, none of it, it doesn't exist, all of it, her bum, her breasts and her snake eyes.

I don't know this but she arrived early, she's looking for me too, scanning the crowd, scouring every corner between the pink buildings, she's too hot under this April sun, she's frightened she invented me, that none of it exists, she's waiting, her stomach hurts. She sees me, harpoons me with her eyes, nothing else exists any more, just our eyes meeting, on the Campo San Bartolomeo, our bodies drawing closer to each other, like magnets, as if possessed.

She gives me a discreet sign, a wink, while my friend's looking away, then she gets up to go to the bathroom. I get up too, claiming I need to make an urgent phone call, I leave my friend immersed in a tourist guide. She's waiting for me against the basin in the toilets. Her lips taste of Campari, her tongue of green olives. She devours me. She whispers at last, at last, at last, at last, at last.

My friend, when we come back red-cheeked and giggling: "Well you took your time!"

27

Before catching her plane she organized a treasure hunt in Venice. She left me messages with clues, riddles and enigmas to solve. I find little presents she's dotted here and there. I give my name at the counter in a patisserie, as instructed. I'm then served freshly squeezed orange juice and jammy biscuits, along with a letter. It's springtime and the light is fiercely beautiful, the sun laps at the canals, the city is intoxicating. She loves me, it's written in black and white. She loves me.

28

She's nearly thirty-five. She's cheerful, irresistibly funny. She's enthusiastic, exhilarating, theatrical. She's amazed by everything, interested in everything. She's always eager to learn. She has a small body, wears size eight clothes. Sometimes size six. She dies of pleasure when she has real Iberico ham. As a general rule, she loves charcuterie, all meat. She's a carnivore. She speaks good Spanish and knows Madrid well but has a special affection

for Italy. One of her favorite things in the world is Brahms'
Piano Trio No. 1. She has no patience with anything.
She wants everything, instantly.

29

She goes on tour with her quartet all over Europe. She
writes to me from Hungary, Belgium, the Netherlands,
Spain, Portugal, Italy and Switzerland. Between tours
she has a few days, sometimes only a few hours, to pop
home, unpack her bag, pack it again, change her scores
and check everything's all right in her apartment. She
skips sorting out her bags, preferring to spend the time
with me. She says it doesn't really matter if she doesn't
go home between two flights, that she'll buy new
clothes in the next city so she has clean things to wear.
She turns up at all hours of day and night, she takes off
her midnight-blue leather jacket, she undresses, she
throws herself onto my bed straight away, she devours
me. The next day she drinks a latte, and nibbles on a
pain au chocolat. She checks the time of her train, or her
plane. She gets dressed. She puts on her leather jacket.
As she leaves with her violin case on her back and her
bag in her hand, she puts her arms around me and bur-
ies her nose in the crook of my neck. She breaks down
and cries every time. Very softly at first, then louder
and louder. She clings to me, she sniffs, she sobs. She

has mascara all over her cheeks, snot on her face. She says she doesn't want this anymore, this life, that it's pointless, that she wants to stay here, go to the cinema, have supper with me in the evenings, do normal things from a normal life. She makes a point of the word *normal*. Her voice is deep suddenly, a disconsolate voice. She strokes my cheek, she kisses me one last time, she leaves mascara on my collar, a smell of midnight-blue leather on my hands. And then, again and again, she leaves.

She comes back. Celebration time all over again. Nights with no sleep, spent talking and making love and starting again until the birds sing. Suppers with wine and cigarettes, too much wine and too many cigarettes, reunions with kisses delayed as long as possible, put off until she can't wait any longer, when she eats my mouth like biting into a cherry. Violently. Wickedly.

30

She loves me. It's written in Venetian ink. Black on white.

31

It's wonderful finding out that she enjoys exactly the same things as me, reading in cafés, eating Japanese food, going to the theater, getting lost in unfamiliar streets, arranging parties. She lives in the Lilas neighborhood, at the end of Line 11. She laughs when I tell her I've become an expert on République station, that I literally fly when I change from Line 8 to Line 11 on my way to her place, because if I miss one Métro it feels as if the world's falling apart, and I can't bear to lose just three minutes of our time together. She meets my daughter, they weigh each other up for a while before getting along passably, and then getting along brilliantly. She sometimes wakes before me, spends time with the child in the kitchen, making breakfast, I find it touching and amusing. It's springtime, life is sweet, I've stopped looking at the magnolias' pale petals when I come out of school. She's waiting for me, as a surprise, hiding in a corner, out of sight of the students. She doesn't know that I now listen only to string quartets, that the minute I have any time to myself I watch videos of her with her quartet on loop, that my favorites are the ones where she plays first violin, where her whole face screws up as she plays, where she looks like a monster.

32

In a medical dictionary. *Latency*: a period of apparent inactivity when symptoms may appear at any time.

33

She doesn't have any children, she doesn't know whether she'd like to have any. She reads extremely slowly, a novel can spend weeks on her bedside table. She wears glasses in the cinema, for driving, sometimes to work on her scores. She has two brothers, both younger. She has a father who passed on his love of ceremony, and a mother who passed on her love of parties. She adores her family. She grew up in the Sixteenth Arrondissement, not very far from the River Seine. She votes left, when she votes.

34

There is just one piece of music I listen to that spring that isn't by a string quartet, "India Song" by Jeanne Moreau. The few opening notes, before her voice comes in, make me cry. When she sings, I sing along with her, my voice hoarse with pain that seems to come from somewhere very deep, pain I can't explain.

Oh, song, you don't really mean anything, but you speak to me of her, you say everything there is to say.

35

A party one evening, in a modern building, an apartment I don't know. Tenth floor, right at the top of a dirty tower block. The lift already reverberates with the boom-boom of overly loud music. Everything shudders. She's wearing too much makeup, as usual. It's nearly summer, she's wearing a long red dress that makes her look bohemian. No one hears when we first ring the bell. She keeps her finger firmly on the buzzer until someone opens the door. Inside the apartment, figures dance in time. Some of her friends are at this party. She introduces me. She says my name, she holds my hand and takes me round the various rooms. She hands me a glass. She drinks. She drinks a lot. She fills my glass every time she fills her own. She's very soon drunk. She dances, scooping up her hair. She looks into my eyes. The rooms have filled with people, there's hardly space enough to dance, it's very hot. She presses herself against me. She doesn't notice my longing for her, crazed, burning, painful. She closes her eyes, opens them again, she looks at me, she dances, she drinks, she dances, she presses herself against me. She smokes cigarettes on the balcony, chatting to people I don't know. She makes an inimitable gesture, tipping off the ash from the top of that tall building. She looks away into the distance, her eyes drunk, her eyes wild, gazing beyond the Ourcq Canal that's visible at the foot of the block. She goes back in to join the party, she drinks, and dances. In the bathroom she kisses me fervently, she moans when I touch her, with the boom-boom pounding endlessly. Everything shudders. She drinks some more, she feels sick. Out on the balcony in the hot air of the middle of the night, she says she wants to go home. She clings to my arm, she's having trouble walking, she's drunk. Blind drunk. No taxi driver agrees to have her in his car. The minute they see her, they say there's no way. She laughs, and cries, she says she's going to be sick. She leans against me. When we get to her apartment, she strips off her bohemian dress. She's naked under it, completely naked. She throws up for a long time, her body racked with convulsions, her forehead in the palm of my hand. Afterward she laughs with relief. She showers and goes to bed. She says she's so sorry, so sorry, so sorry, she ruined everything, she'll understand if I ever leave her, after what's just happened. She doesn't get it at all. To me she's even more desirable than before.

36

I go home to my place alone, by Métro. My whole body quivering. Days go by, weeks go by, soft green buds just keep on opening on branches silhouetted like lace against sky-blue skies. Not a cloud, ever. Blue in every direction, with Japanese-cherry pink on every street corner. Pools of sunlight on pavements. No gloominess, anywhere. Just joy. This spring is a party that goes on and on. My body can't get over it. Change in general state of health, again and again. I go up my street, walking more and more quickly, I go through my front door, slam it when I close it. I rummage through my bookcase, eventually dig out the dictionary, leaf feverishly through its pages and, slightly embarrassed, I finally find and read out loud – for my own benefit – the definition of the word *passion*.

37

She just wears G-strings. Hardly ever a bra. For sleeping she has a selection of baby-doll nighties, including a devastatingly sexy black one in silk-like fabric. She always has a bottle of water on her, she gets very thirsty, she drinks as if her life depends on it, with her eyes closed, not taking a breath. She can sometimes drink a whole bottle down in one. She does a lot of things as if her life depends on them.

38

She rears up over me, her breasts proud and bare, and beautiful, tragically beautiful. Time stretches elastically, almost stops. Everything becomes slow and long. My heart prances in my chest, in my veins, in my temples. Kneeling next to me, she looks like an icon, a religious image. It's almost as if she's praying. She's not touching me. She's caressing me with her gaze. A brief blessed pause. A sacred moment. Silence. Then she looks into my eyes and drives her fingers into me, deep, very deep, so deep it makes my head spin, my eyes close. She breathes on my eyelids, her mouth very close to mine. She whispers words of love that cut right through me. Her fingers are deep, lost inside me, deep in my belly she plays a music that drives me crazy. She makes my body contort, my back arch, she never stops. She goes deeper and deeper, faster and faster, until I'm just a rag doll, a puppet.

39

Pantin, Romainville and Bagnolet are neighboring towns of the Les Lilas commune, which was created on 24 July 1867 and comprised some of their land. There were plans to call the new commune Napoléon-le-Bois or Commune-de-Padoue, in reference to the Duke of Padua who once lived there. In the end the commune's name was chosen for the flower-filled gardens that covered the hill during the Second Empire. Until the law of 10 July 1964, Les Lilas was part of the Seine region. It now comes under Seine-Saint-Denis after an administrative transfer that came into effect on 1 January 1968.

The town is close to Porte des Lilas station on the Paris Métro, and is served by Mairie des Lilas station on Line 11. It has a population of 22,762. Its postal code is 93260. Its inhabitants are called Lilasiens. Sarah lives on rue de la Liberté.

The town's motto is: "I was a flower, I am a city."

40

In the mornings she just can't let me go to work. Once my daughter's been dropped off at school, she gets on the bus next to me, with her violin on her back. She walks in step with me down the street that runs along the front of the Fifteenth Arrondissement's *Mairie*. She's lighthearted, talking nonsense, laughing about everything. She dips into a brown paper bag for fistfuls of cherries and gobbles them uninhibitedly. She thinks it's funny that I get embarrassed when she comes too close to me, when her hand tries to catch hold of mine. She says oh it's fine who gives a damn about your students, we're educating them, that's a good thing, isn't it. She eats her cherries as she walks along and spits the pips out onto the street. She says oh it's fine do you really think your colleagues haven't seen lesbians before. She pushes me into the lobby of a building. She presses the button for the lift, she pulls me by the arm when it arrives. She smacks her mouth against mine when I say this isn't very responsible, I'm going to be late and we can't do this. She says seeing as you don't want me to kiss you outside your school, I've got to find somewhere. She chooses the top floor, the eleventh. There's wall-to-wall carpeting, neatly lined-up doors, slightly muffled bursts of conversation coming from around us. She pushes me up against the wall, strokes my teeth with her tongue, bruises my breasts with her fingers. She smells of blue leather and thundering desire.

During a dinner, when it's raining outside, a soft summer rain, she tells some friends what *con fuoco* means in a score. She waves her arms around as she speaks. She herself becomes the fire, the soul-spinning impetuosity. She looks like a demon. She's drop-dead beautiful, to-die-for hot.

She drinks a lot. She smokes, one cigarette after another. She's got a way of looking me in the eye when she's smoking that sends an agonizing thunderbolt through my body. It hurts that I want her so much, that I so long to tip her back onto a bed, undo the button on her trousers and bring my mouth to the source of my wonderment. She puts a hand on the back of my neck when I caress her snatch with my tongue, she instills a movement in me, it starts with her hips and makes me dizzy, it obliterates everything around us.

41

She's six and a half years old, she's waiting for me outside the school with a *pain au chocolat* and a little girl's grin. She drags me along to concerts and to dinners on restaurant terraces with her friends. She follows me everywhere, takes me everywhere, she doesn't leave my side, won't let me out of her sight. She wakes me with fingers in the very depths of me, the first signs of long sun-filled days. She never tires of having her body against mine. Her audacity borders on irreverence. She asks for more salmon with her *chirashi* in a Japanese restaurant on the rue Monsieur-le-Prince. She uses a completely different voice to say for God's sake I ordered a salmon *chirashi*, and I've basically got just rice, can you explain that. She pretends not to notice that I'm sitting there opposite her, flushed scarlet with shame. She winks at me when the waiter comes back with a plate full of magnificent slices of fresh salmon. She clinks her glass against mine to toast this free feast. She says here's to you, my love, and to this orgy of salmon. She roars with laughter at the Comédie-Française, in the upper circle, far too loudly for such a beautiful setting. She couldn't care less about decorum, or good manners. She's alive.

Passion. From the Latin *patior*, to experience, endure, suffer. Feminine noun. With the notion of protracted or successive suffering: the action of suffering. With the notion of excess, exaggeration, intensity: love as an irre-sistible and violent inclination toward a single object, sometimes descending into obsession, entailing a loss of moral compass and of critical faculties, and liable to compromise mental stability. In Scholasticism, what is experienced by an individual, the thing with which he or she is associated or to which he or she is subjugated.

42

She offers me a ticket, in the upper circle at the Comédie-Française. The play is *A Midsummer Night's Dream*.

43

She hung up on me, furious, with tears in her voice. A few hours later she manages to get into the school, I don't really know how. She comes to find me in the room where I'm working, sitting at a table, covering books, concentrating to be sure I do it well and the adhesive paper doesn't leave any air pockets on the covers. She has a paper bag full of apricots. She glances round the room. She sits down next to me, she doesn't say a word. She settles for diving her hand into the bag periodically, taking out an apricot and opening it between her nails, with a deft, precise, almost irritable flick. She brings the fruit to her mouth and doesn't offer me any, not once. She piles the stones on top of each other in a funny lopsided construction that nearly collapses every time we move. She doesn't say a thing. She looks pigheaded. Later, when nearly an hour has elapsed in silence and she has fruit juice over her wrists, she whispers almost inaudibly I think I love you too much.

44

She has nits because my daughter caught them at school. She takes things in hand, laughs at me because I'm horrified, she buys nit lotion, does machine after machine full of washing, with the sheets from my place and the sheets from her place, she says don't worry, it's nothing, they'll go. When she's with me I don't worry.

She sets out from my apartment at about eight in the evening to meet up with friends. When she leaves them, at three-ish in the morning, she calls me to pick up one or other of the conversations we left dangling. She doesn't realize that she's exhausting herself, and exhausting me.

William Shakespeare's *A Midsummer Night's Dream* is an unclassifiable play, which features a combination of comedy and magic from start to finish. The text reflects on the power of imagination in the face of arbitrary laws, particularly the rigors of family law. Night – a time of disorder, dreams and fantasies – is balanced with day – a time of reality, order and discipline.

45

June passes swiftly and July stretches out over the course of my first holidays as a teacher, grenadine cordials on café terraces and the football World Cup. Off in the distance she hops from foot to foot in the chill of Mont-parnasse station in the early hours. She gets to know my family home, between lake and ocean. On the first evening, the lake – a sublime place – has saved her a special welcome, shimmering in the last vestiges of sunlight. The next day, after a few grilled sardines gobbled down as we sat beside the sea, she watches as I'm bowled over by malicious waves, and laughs at how much I love it, as I always have, how much I love this, being thrown onto the jagged rocks and sharp little shells, launching straight back on the attack, falling, getting up, and falling again. She can't get over the way I spend hours in huge waves, turned over and over by their overbearing power. She watches me lose my footing, go under, stop thinking about anything, letting myself be buffeted, spun round, buffeted again, and staying there for hours in this des-potic imperious surging, with saltwater all the way down my throat, my eyes closed and my fists balled. At night she tells me about the fears she's had since childhood, fears that define her. She whispers under the thick quilt.

46

She goes off on tour with her quartet. She leaves me drained. She writes to say join me, I'm dying without you. She writes come, I'm waiting for you, life has no meaning when you're not here. She writes I'm playing at the Château de Chambord, it's so beautiful here, go on, come and join me. She doesn't know that I thrill at these words, that I pack my bag within the hour, jump onto obscure trains, undertaking a seven-hour journey that starts with a cappuccino at the Arrivals bar. At Montceau-les-Mines station, where stray dogs stray between dense tufts of soft green grass, I read about Yann Andréa's death in a copy of *Libération* picked up from a bench. 14:59, still four more hours till I get there. In the heat that blurs the rails at Moulins-sur-Allier station, eating a ham sandwich and drinking lemonade seem to be exactly the right things to do as I screw up my eyes on the deserted platform and embark on a Hervé Guibert book I've never read, *Les Aventures singulières*. She writes oh come quickly my darling quickly my love I'm pining for you I need your skin. At Saint-Pierre-des-Corps I run frantically to make my next connection. The sun's going down, I've been traveling since dawn. At Blois station I take a taxi to Chambord. I'm dumbstruck by the sight of the château, which suddenly appears around a bend in a tree-lined drive. She writes we're starting our scales, we're playing Franck's quintet, it's so beautiful, I can't wait for you to hear it. I run over the gravel up to the château, my bag slung across my body. There she is, in the distance, a tiny figure, walking carefully over the empty, abandoned lawn in her concert shoes, her high-heeled shoes, in her very distinguished long black dress. She hugs me, she inhales my panting breath between her lips. She reigns over Chambord, she dominates my heart, she governs my life. She's a queen.

47

In the hunting lodge in the middle of the night – after the concert, after the social niceties – she lies me down on the narrow single bed in her room, she licks the inside of my wrists for a long time, she stifles my cries with her hand, she eats my whole body, and every place she touches keeps the moist trace of her mouth and the smell of her saliva all night. On the train to Paris the next day she has a work meeting with the rest of her quartet. I'm sitting a little way away, and she often looks up at me and smiles, she smiles a smile that imprints itself in me like a tattoo.

48

The summer spools by like this. When we're together life goes too quickly, hurtling past. She runs – and I run along behind her – through the corridors of the Métro, to catch trains on time, to meet up when she comes home. She walks – and I walk along behind her – through the streets of Paris that we explore tirelessly, she jumps onto the pillars at the Colonnes de Buren art installation, she's a child, she's wowed by the color of clouds, she's a child. I'm in love with a child. She scuttles into the bathroom and I scuttle in behind her, behind the shower curtain where I wash her body as if washing something sacred. She stands up straight and I stand behind her, looking at the departures board, when she goes away again. In this new life that I'm leading along-side hers, there are stations and trains, but not for me, never. It's all about that. So trains the whole time, then: trains to catch, trains on time, chock-full trains, night trains, late trains. There are airports, planes, boarding schedules, landing schedules, carousels for collecting luggage; there are taxis, Métros and changing on the Métro. Not for me, then, ever. I accompany her, at a run, short of breath, we've shared the bags between us and we often race onto the platform just a minute before the departure, but sometimes we don't, sometimes we have time for a long kiss before that familiar ding sound. Departures; there I am with my reassuring words *have a good trip, use the journey to get some rest*, my stupid words *don't forget me* or maybe *write to me, promise you will, promise you'll write*, there I am coming out with words that I mostly communicate with my eyes, and my lips formulate the most ridiculous *love you* shapes of my adult life, there I am making heart shapes with my fingers, I step forward slightly when the train sets off, not taking my eyes off hers, there I am laughing at her antics through the window, and then I stop and, with my hands in my pockets, I go back to the city that's carried on with its life. Arrivals; there I am waiting on the platform, my heart pounding, looking out for her face, noticing in passing what other people look like, all those other people, and not one of them interests me, I look out for her and hop up and down impatiently, I want everything, instantly, the shape of her, her smile, her eyes, her perfume, her mouth. Often the arrival is in the evening and the departure the next morning. Often within the space of twenty-four hours we meet up on a platform at one station and say our goodbyes on a platform at another. Sometimes it's the same station. That's how life goes that summer.

49

In a restaurant where my parents have taken me to celebrate my first year as a teacher, I blush and tell them I'm in love with a woman. They say oh right and what's her name.

50

She joins me in a house straight out of a fairy tale, a place that belongs to some friends of mine, in the depths of the Aveyron region. She's stunned by the vegetable garden, by the caravan in the field where we take our siestas, with her nose against mine. She shivers when a storm rolls in. She shivers when I read her an erotic passage by Hervé Guibert. She runs a bath for me, she dries my hair, she kisses my cheeks wetted with tears when I'm miserable at the thought of her leaving again soon, already. She watches me make a risotto with lemon, with mint, with onions, with hazelnuts. Under the flowery sheet in the bedroom suffused with a blueish light, she makes love to me tirelessly. She runs through the rain with her jacket over her head to go and buy lubricant at the pharmacy. She comes back, laughing uproariously, mimicking the woman's face when she said what she needed. She says what a bitch I mean what a bitch she wouldn't have given a damn if I'd bought condoms. She puts vinyls on the record player, she insists that we learn the boogie-woogie, she finds dance instruction videos and we watch them, laughing, we go out into the street to have more space to dance, it's three o'clock, four o'clock in the morning. On the square in that Aveyron village she holds up her arms and beats out the time, one two three ba-ba-da, one two three ba-ba-da, she corrects me, left leg, and ba-ba-da, and ba-ba-da, she lights cigarettes, she has sweat between her breasts, she laughs, she says it's funny I never feel tired with you, the nights are even better than our days.

51

In the deserted house I listen to Beethoven's quartet, Opus 130, over and over again. Stale coffee slithers like a black octopus over the chipped porcelain of the chipped sink where I drown my sorrows by doing the washing-up. Still on the table are two cigarettes, forgotten in the rush of leaving, still here are her soft fingerings, here, just here. Thanks to the phenomenon known as persistence of vision, my retinas turn the cracked walls of this house into white screens for a shadow puppet of her.

52

The intensity of our connection is too strong, storms erupt. She turns nasty, she screams till the walls shake, she falls to her knees, racked with heartrending sobs. She gets back up, staggers, comes to nestle in my arms, apologizes. One word too many and she starts shrieking again, saying this can't go on this can't go on, and slamming doors. She lets me catch up with her at the last minute, she doesn't fight when I undress her and force her to get into the bath where I wash her meticulously under the astonished eye of the resident cat, she cries silently while I go shhhhh between my teeth, shhhhh like someone soothing a teething child or a strapping man felled by fever or an old man preparing to die, come on, shhhhh, it's over, there, shhhhh.

Ludwig van Beethoven's String Quartet No. 13 in B-flat major, Opus 130, was completed in December 1825 and published before the composer's death. It has six movements and originally ended with the *Grosse Fuge*. But, faced with the bafflement of audiences and on the insistence of his editor, Beethoven resolved to separate the fugue from the rest of the quartet. In the autumn of 1826 he composed a substitute finale, which remains his last finished work. The Cavatina that serves as the fifth movement is considered the dramatic highpoint of the work and one of the most poignant melodies Beethoven ever wrote. Most present-day performances of this quartet revert to using the *Grosse Fuge* as the finale because the Cavatina's dramatic intensity is too powerful and needs this liberating conclusion.

53

In mid-August she flies off to Istanbul for six days, which feels like an eternity to us. She calls me every day. She describes the city, a place I already know but discover all over again through her words. She tells me when she's playing the violin alone in the apartment while her traveling companions are out strolling along the Bosporus. She seems disappointed when I say I won't be there when she flies home. It doesn't occur to her that this is a ploy of mine. She arrives, looking rather tired, she doesn't suspect I'm here at the airport, she doesn't suspect that I've been here for hours already, pacing like a tiger in a cage, having drunk coffees from every available machine in Terminal B, having studied and studied again the arrivals board, the metal doors and the faces of travelers. She doesn't know I'm watching her as she says goodbye to her traveling companions, that I'm scrutinizing every part of her body, and her face, that I laugh to see her laugh, that my whole body shudders at the thought of holding her close any minute. She jumps back when I pop up right next to her, she drops her bag, throws her arms around my neck and dissolves into tears. She intertwines her legs with mine in the taxi taking us to her apartment, to her bed, her bower in Les Lilas, her lilac town. She sets off again on tour very early the next morning. She grabs my hand to run through the corridors of the Gare de Lyon. She's late, as usual, she just couldn't get up on time after a night of all-consuming lovemaking. Even so, she stops by the station's piano and, with her violin on her back, standing in the middle of the crowd, she starts to play a syrupy tune from the eighties, striking the notes without looking at them, not looking at them because it's me she's looking at. I'm embarrassed and I'm proud, she looks me right in the eye and, standing there in the middle of the crowd, she sings – loudly, at the top of her lungs – dreams are my reality.

54

It's all about that, it's all about Sarah the unknown woman, Sarah the honorable maiden, Sarah the prudent lady, Sarah the extravagant woman, Sarah the bizarre woman. Sarah the lone woman.

55

The telephone rings just once unanswered and then the hold music starts up. It's Vivaldi. *The Four Seasons*. Summer. A man's voice eventually says hello, Paris emergency service. He listens in silence while I describe what's happening to me, the persistent sharp pain in my chest, on the left-hand side, spreading through my left arm so that I almost can't move it. The voice on the other end asks me a number of specific questions, tells me to make several movements. The man seems astonished. He says hold the line, I'm going to speak to the duty doctor. I hear him put down the headset, his heavy footsteps lumber away in my ear, I wait, I can hear other telephone operators also asking questions, I keep waiting, a good while. The footsteps come back. The man's voice says hello, it says hello, Miss, are you in a relationship at the moment, do you think that what you actually have is an aching heart, or maybe, you know, a heavy heart?

She writes come and join me it's still summer here. She writes I can't take sunshine and heat without you, I hear the cicadas every morning but I want to wake up with you. She writes get off at Avignon station, I'll come and pick you up by car, I'll manage somehow, come on my love, it's too complicated when we're apart. She doesn't know that I thrill at these words, that I pack my bag within the hour, that I jump onto the first train to Avignon. She's waiting for me on the platform, in an implausible bright-red dress, she's well dressed for once, well dressed with neat hair, not at all thrown together, she's bought me a coffee, she wants to show me an article about her quartet in a magazine, she doesn't do it on purpose but she steals the magazine, she forgets to pay the newsagent, so exhilarated that we're together again, she comes out of the shop with the magazine under her arm, it makes her laugh, a great loud laugh, then she asks me what's this about a pain in your chest, you're not doing breast cancer on us, are you, she laughs again, at her marvelous joke, I mumble no it's nothing actually it's already gone, she almost runs to the car and I run after her, the car is scorching from sitting in unforgiving sun, which beats down straight and hard, she opens the windows and lurches off before fastening her seatbelt, she howls with laughter as she does a bonkers U-turn in the car park, at the sound of the tires squealing, she says I'm going fast so they don't come after us for the magazine, we *are* thieves after all, she heads toward Arles, she sighs when I run my hand up her thigh, when I push aside the two halves of the bright-red dress to stroke her where she's her softest, her tenderest, at the top of her thighs, she closes her eyes for a fraction of a second when I put my finger into her wet snatch, she bites her lip when I put in a second finger, she puts her foot on the accelerator and comes, with the windows open, at ninety kilometers an hour, in the stifling heat of the car and the relentless, maddening song of cicadas.

56

The cool temperature in the abbey is a relief, as if the old stones graciously make a point of refreshing whoever steps into this sacred place. She's rehearsing with her seven associates. She told me they were playing an octet, she explained this in the crumpled sheets of dawn and I didn't really listen, dazzled by the sight of her naked body in the sunlight filtering through the shutters. She's first violin. She glances at me often, and I look back from where I'm sitting in the cloisters, reading Hervé Guibert. The abbey fills with people, they shuffle up on the small wooden benches, she messages join me in the dressing room, she opens the door and I discover a beehive of frenetic activity, the girls checking themselves in the mirror, hard-faced as they apply mascara or a last dab of lipstick, the only boy is buttoning up his shirt while nibbling on a piece of fruit, everyone's joshing, quips ping back and forth. She asks me to do up her dress, to say if her bun is okay. She says go on, go back out, you'll lose your seat, and she's right, there are no seats left by the time I get there, I park myself by one of the pillars in the cloisters, sheltered under these centuries-old stones, they walk onstage, she comes out first, she's holding her violin and bow in the same hand, she stops, she waits for the other seven to be onstage, they bow, they move their instruments into position, there's a pause, two or three seconds of nothingness, of coughs from the audience and then everyone holds their breath. She looks at her fellow players, she inhales deeply and throws herself headlong into the music.

57

She's surprised by my instant obsession with this octet, by the way I want to listen to it the whole time, on repeat if need be, to listen to every available recording. She doesn't know that seeing her play the fourth movement was one of the most beautiful things in my life. She has no idea about my feverish palms, my palpitating pulse, voices around me growing hazy. And then sudden silence, the bright light onstage, the harsh heartless light. The momentary pause, all at once dark, all at once silent. And nothing. For a few moments nothing. Except for my palpitating pulse. And then. And then she comes onstage. Everyone, all around me, everyone claps. I don't hear a thing. I look at her. Her long dress. The glint of her earrings. The gleam of her front teeth. My vampire. Her violin. Her bun. Her faraway look. My dispossessed breathing. The score she opens. Her eyelashes when she sits down. In that deafening silence. Mendelssohn's octet, and her right there. As first violin. Eight bodies, thirty-two strings, everything motionless. Nothing moving. Life frozen. It'll go on for a hundred years, like in fairy tales. But no. A tilt of her chin and everything bubbles over. She's a flame surging into life throughout the *allegro*. She jumps, my wild child does, she leaps and hops and flares. *Con fuoco*, and I'm not the one saying that. It's not her violin trilling now, it's Sarah herself. I wish it could go on for a hundred years, like in fairy tales, I wish it would never stop. And then during the *presto* she puffs out her chest, my little soldier does, she goes off to war and I'm her captive, my feet and wrists bound. It's the closing bars, she looms taller, arches her back, becomes a titan. Everything quivers, everything explodes. There with her proud breasts, she postures and triumphs. She looks like someone setting off on a journey. She's going off to war. Doesn't know when she'll be back.

She doesn't know that her mother, who was there at the abbey, saw me leaning against the pillar in the cloister, with eyes only for her daughter, burning from the inside with admiration and desire, and that her mother, who didn't know me, thought to herself that the world as she knew it had just changed for ever.

58

She often takes off her sandals, with a flick of her ankles, to drive barefoot. Afterward the soles of her feet are black from the pedals. She prefers showering in the morning to the evening. She played badminton for many years. When she's ill she finds it difficult swallowing pills, she pulls faces and shakes her head to get them down her throat. She uses outdated expressions, improbable and ridiculously uncool words. She can't really dance, she dances very badly even.

59

She says don't give a fuck, I'll tell them, I'm so happy with you that I want to shout it to the whole world from the rooftops. She says they're my parents, they love me so they'll be happy that I'm happy, that's what being a parent means, isn't it. She says look, your parents reacted so well. She says and anyway everyone knows now, your daughter, my brothers, our friends, I can't keep hiding it from them. Off she goes without a care to have supper with her parents, leaving me with a strange foreboding in my heart. She calls me a few hours later, she can't get her words out she's crying so violently down the phone, she begs me can I come over to your place, she falls into my arms when I open the door to my apartment, she says my darling it was horrendous it was the worst day of my life they were foul my father doesn't want to see me again. It's all about that, the fact we can't love, drink and sing in peace, and if we want to live happily we have to live in hiding.

The Four Seasons are the four concertos for violin, composed by Antonio Vivaldi, that open the collection called *Il cimento dell'armonia e dell'invenzione.* The contest between harmony and invention. *L'estate*, summer, has an *allegro*, an *adagio,* and a *presto* that abruptly interrupts the *adagio*. Vivaldi's note as a directive for this last movement is *tempo impetuoso*.

60

Autumn comes with no warning. She turns up with masses of pastries, she says come on, my darlings, we're off to the market. She kisses me, she offers to make a big salad, she wants to make love all the time, absolutely all the time. The only time she lets me sleep is when I'm ill. She dreams up picnics for the three of us in the park near my apartment. She looks at her diary, she says I'm going away on tour a lot, we're hardly going to see each other before Christmas. She looks devastated. When I come out of my new school she's waiting for me with a rose in her hand or a *pain au chocolat* or a book wrapped in pretty paper with words of love written on it. She comes to my friends' parties with me. She arranges dinners with her friends at Les Lilas. She drops by to have lunch with me, she brings sandwiches and a brown paper bag full to bursting with very ripe plums, we sit down on the pavement in a slightly hidden street in the suburb where I work to gobble down our royal feast. She kisses me with plum juice still in the corners of her mouth. She's alive. She doesn't realize that nothing matters to me now except the time I spend with her, that I'm feeling depressed, that I don't like my work anymore, that I'll get my doctor to give me a sicknote as soon as I can.

61

In Brussels she falls asleep on the grass and I watch her sleep for a long time, relieved that her love for me is on pause for a moment, relieved that she's stopped talking at last, that she's stopped dashing about. In Helsinki she buys herself a long gray cashmere coat, she walks all around the twilit city like a little gray riding hood, I walk behind her thinking it's actually me who's the little girl and she's the wolf, yes, that's it, she'll end up devouring me.

62

One Sunday she's playing at the Théâtre des Champs-Élysées. She's terrified, for the first time since I've known her. The concert is sublime and she is exquisitely graceful. She doesn't even catch my eye at the end because I'm in such a hurry to avoid meeting her parents. She doesn't know how furiously happy it makes me when later in the day, after her mandatory social lunch, she joins me at my parents' house in the suburbs at siesta time. She huddles up to me in the spare-room bed. I struggle to believe I'm hugging the girl who was up on that prestigious stage a few hours earlier.

She's moved by Niki de Saint Phalle. Her lips taste of wasabi when I kiss her as we come out of a Japanese restaurant on the boulevard de Rochechouart. She asks me to wait for her at the Palais-Royal, I spot a restaurant called the Entracte, the interval, I wait a long time for her, I'm worried she won't come, that it's over, I panic for no reason. When she finally arrives, she finds me in tears.

She devours me. She wants to make love all the time. She instigates arguments, increasingly violent ones. She bites me. Straight afterward she suggests watching a François Truffaut film. She chooses *Bed and Board*.

63

She's going on tour to Japan with the quartet. She opens the presents I hand her and finds a paperback edition of *Hiroshima, Mon Amour* and notebooks of blank staves. She smiles when I say I'd like her to write music, that I see her future as even greater than her current success. Her snake eyes give me a fizzing feeling in my stomach when I tell her that if she dies tomorrow I don't want anyone to forget her. And I'll make sure they don't.

On the other side of the world she becomes a shadow on my computer screen. She looks like a ghost when we talk at impossible times of day, for her just as much as for me, because the time difference is so restrictive. Her body moves but her face stays motionless, she looks like a Picasso, a zombie. She calls me from one hotel room after another. In Tokyo she undresses, very slowly, in front of the camera. Her breasts look unreal on the screen. Her breasts are what I like best, her supple little breasts, softer than anything I've found anywhere else. She strokes her body, it's torture and it's wonderful. She comes, all those kilometers away from me, with her mouth open and her eyes closed, my ghost who's very much alive. When she returns it's December. She can't believe a year has gone by since we met at that starchy apartment. She wants to organize a big party, with a mixture of our friends. It's a success. In her apartment in Les Lilas, people dance till dawn. The next day she starts a fight over breakfast. She screams and shouts right in my face. She frightens me. She scratches the skin off my arm with her nails when she tries to hold me back as I jump into a taxi, to put an end to it. She doesn't know that I'm bleeding, that I never want to see her again.

She has a cousin who works at the Paris Opera and who shows us around the workshops where they make the scenery. A little door leads onto the stage. Sarah goes through it, and I follow her, enveloped in a bitter yet powdery smell. No noise, apart from a few muffled sounds, the footsteps of stage technicians, people talking in the wings. Up on that stage, facing the silent empty seats, she looks so small. Helpless. Harmless.

64

She goes away again. She leaves me to myself, and a life I'm no longer interested in. She goes away again, delighted to be back with her fellow performers, with the subtle fear before each concert and the jokes afterward.

She just leaves me there with my heart dangling uselessly. She doesn't know that I listen to Mendelssohn's octet on loop, at a loose end, lying on my bed, my soul suffering. She goes away again. She snaps closed bags that she's packed in a hurry, without a single look at me, as I sit on the other side of the bed. She runs around the whole apartment looking for a particular score, a particular pair of panties. She loses everything, she gets annoyed. She can't wait to catch her train. She leaves me to my own devices, to my responsibilities as a mother and a good teacher. She couldn't care less.

Bed and Board is a French film – *Domicile conjugal* – written and directed by François Truffaut and released in 1970. Running time: 100 minutes. The cast includes Jean-Pierre Léaud, Claude Jade and Hiroko Berghauer. It's a sequel to *Stolen Kisses*, released in 1968. The trilogy of Antoine Doinel's adventures ended later, in 1979, with the release of *Love on the Run*.

65

Sometimes she goes mad. Mad with fury then mad with misery. She screams, throws herself at me and scratches my face, with a monstrous expression on hers. She's worse than a witch in a fairy tale. She resents me, for everything, for stealing her time, stealing her youth, stealing her family's love, stealing the idea she's had since childhood of how she should live her life. She doesn't say it but I can hear it, it rings in my ears, thief, thief, thief. She gets angry with me for silly little things, all sorts of things, but deep down, I can tell, she's angry with me for existing, for coming into her life, she's angry with me for being a woman. She resents me because she can't suddenly just love me in peace. She flies into blazing tempers, unforgettable tempers. Her little body is transformed. She looks like an animal, a furious animal, she roars, flushed red all over. And in the heat of the moment she forgets the Venetian love, the hidden kisses, the endless fondling. The remedy for these mad paroxysms is always the same. I wait for a momentary lull and force her to undress. Once she's naked, I try to concentrate on what I need to do. She carries on shouting while I push her under the shower, with her hair hanging over her eyes. She lets herself be maneuvered, quietens a little when the water starts to flow over her. I soap her, starting with her feet, easing my hands up over her calves, trying to stop the spasms in her legs. I stand on tiptoe and hold the shower over her head, getting water everywhere, I'm soaked, the floor's soaked, the bathmat's soaked, she moans under the flow of hot water, her anger starts to subside, she lets me turn off the water to massage her head with shampoo, gently and then more firmly, my jaw hurts from clamping my teeth together, I talk to her inside my head, I say you're going to calm down for goodness' sake, aren't you, you're going to stop, I talk to her in the shower, I say come on it's over my love it's over, it's okay, you see, it's going to be okay, I take her out, I move her body around as best I can, I rub her briskly, I roll her up in a towel and sit her on the side of the bath, she's still sniveling a bit but the storm has passed, I turn on the hairdryer and, slowly, patiently, I brush her hair till it's dry. She lets herself be led over to the bed where she collapses, where I anoint her body with cream, slowly, trying not to wake the wild animal with a sudden move or a misunderstood word. She lets herself be buried under the duvet, her face swollen from too much crying. I close the door to the apartment without a sound, and I go out into the street and howl at the top of my lungs, my fists balled, like a wolf on the night of a full moon, I howl until my throat burns, I howl for this vanishing love.

66

Hiroshima, My Love is the screenplay of Alain Resnais' film, written by Marguerite Duras, published by Gallimard. First published: 1960. When the film was released and Duras heard that the French Ministry for Foreign Affairs opposed its selection for the Cannes Film Festival, she wrote in an open letter: "We wanted to make a film about love. We wanted to depict the worst conditions of love, the most frequently criticized, the most reprehensible, the most unacceptable conditions." The connection between love and death that lies at the heart of *Hiroshima, Mon Amour* is a recurring theme in Marguerite Duras' work. As in *The Lover*, the book that won her the Goncourt Prize, love is doomed to fail.

She looks at me. Her eyes are hard, behind her glasses. Hard but thoughtful. She looks at me, Marguerite does. Marguerite Duras, on the poster for the exhibition we went to together. It says *exhibition* on the poster. It says *15 October–12 January*, near the glasses worn by Marguerite, who looks at me tenderly. It's all about that, it's all about Sarah drifting between the lines of Marguerite's writing. That was the winter before. It says *portrait of a writing process* on the poster. It says *Duras Song* on the poster. That was the name of the exhibition. She looks at me thoughtfully. What are you thinking, Marguerite? Do you remember last winter, when she and I wandered the streets? Are you singing, Marguerite? It says *Duras Song* on the poster. Duras dreams up her enduring song, a midwinter night's dream-song.

In *Hiroshima, Mon Amour*:
HER: I didn't make anything up.
HIM: You made it all up.

67

She still sometimes waits for me outside the school, a little less frequently than before. She takes the child to school with me in the mornings. She laughs at how hard I find it to get up, she says I'm a bear, her grumpy bear. She likes eating Japanese, almost every other evening. She likes eating a square of chocolate in the evenings with her herbal tea. Dark, preferably. She has an incredibly soft bum and I have trouble not touching it when we're together. In bed, it's even more difficult. In the morning she likes making love still half asleep.

68

Winter's back. She says she doesn't like this time of year. One morning when she needs to get up terribly early to go off on tour, we step outside into great big snowflakes. It's all about that, very early one morning on a black January night, the orangey light of the street lamps, the dark streets of Les Lilas, Sarah's silhouette, her silhouette as I know it, with her violin case on her back and her skinny little legs underneath, her suitcase dragged along by her right arm, a hood over her head. She opens her mouth slightly, to catch snowflakes on her tongue, she laughs, her nose is red, she has white on her eyelashes, she looks at me and says breathtaking isn't it my love. To celebrate this, she insists we wait till the bakery opens, bang on six o'clock, she dives inside and emerges triumphantly with two *pains au chocolat*. It's all about that, life being dazzling whatever the circumstances. We run to catch the Métro and, warm at last in the train as it pulls away, we bite into our pastries with freezing hands and running noses.

She insists on coming on holiday with my daughter and me. She doesn't know that I'd rather go away alone, that I'm exhausted by this relationship, by having her in my life. On the night train she has the berth opposite mine, on the top bunks. She leaves her little light on. When the child goes to sleep, just underneath us on a middle bunk, she gradually peels the SNCF sheet away from her body, she looks me in the eye, and slowly fondles her breasts.

69

It's a spring like any other, a spring to depress the best of us. A year has gone by, a year of music, a year of shudders, a year of sulfur and suffering. She says she wants to leave me, that this life we have is too tempestuous, it's like a storm. The captain's leaving the ship. She doesn't know that I cry in my shower every morning, that I have stomachaches every evening, that I can't sleep without sleeping pills now. She says I'm the love of her life, her one and only love, she says she doesn't know what she should do, carry on with this weird complicated life or forget about it all, she says our love is the most magical and the most terrible thing that's happened to her. She says she can't choose, that it's a problem, in life. She decides to keep passion at arm's length, she says we can try seeing each other just twice a week, leaving gaps between the periods of madness, to make life less jarring, less stormy.

She can be wonderful, she runs baths for me, she massages my back, makes delicious meals for me, comes with me to important meetings, she tells me I'm her freedom, her respite, her little breath of fresh air. She can be poisonous, she's stopped replying when I message her, she's monosyllabic, makes sure she's not available, she says I'm stifling her, that she needs to breathe, breathe, breathe.

She wakes up feeling very hungry, she takes a feline stretch and says we must go out for a delicious breakfast. She wants to go for a walk afterward so she opts for Angelina's, near the Tuileries Garden. She's quiet, almost listless in the uber-chic tea room. There might as well be a black hole between us. She eats her toast without a sound, without any thundering laughter, without an anecdote for me. She barely smiles when I clown around to amuse her. She gets up to go to the toilet, without a word, without a backward glance at me. She's startled when she senses me behind her. In the big gilt mirror in Angelina's ladies' toilets – up on the first floor, with views of the garden – she finally smiles at my reflection when I press her up against the basin to make love to her in silence, a quickie, with her skirt hitched up against the immaculate white enamel. Her sighs of pleasure are no consolation.

70

She was truly passionate about cars as a teenager. She knew an incredible number of different models. She had a particular fondness for Renaults. She adored the Renault 5, but also really liked the Renault 25 and, even more so, the Renault 21, which she thought less grandiloquent and sententious than the 25, and which she deemed especially modern. Her favorite model was incontestably the Alpine A110, almost a racing car. She can count at astonishing speed, she's incredibly good at mental arithmetic. Her spelling is pretty much perfect. But she still stubbornly insists on putting a rogue circumflex on the *o* of *idiom*. She's not frightened of much but she has two major phobias, moths and statues, any statue. She can't stay in a room if there's a moth in it. She says she can't stand how unpredictable they are, how she never knows where they're going next, they're temperamental, disturbing and changeable. With statues, she quakes at the thought of them suddenly coming to life. Switching from being dead to being alive.

She's as beautiful as a Bonnard nude. She's as pink and yellow as his pinks and yellows, as affecting as the women he painted, as delicate and as fragile. She could be my model if I could paint. She would pose for me, in all sorts of different lights, she'd always be more beautiful than in the previous painting. She'd be the ideal woman, a mysterious, glorious woman, an icon.

She looks at the scar on my body left by the cesarean. She doesn't say anything, but runs a finger along the white line just above my thick dark hairs, and wipes away my tears with her other hand, she whispers that she thinks I'm beautiful, she doesn't know that it doesn't comfort me, that I wish my beauty could match hers. She's like a character in a novel. She doesn't see that it's painful, for the people close to her. She's alive.

71

She laughs with delight when she realizes that I've lied to her, that we're not going to the theater but to the Gare de Lyon to catch a train to Marseille. She asks me how long I've been planning this surprise, she wants to know all the details, how did I arrange it, contacting the quartet, and then her family, whom she was meant to be spending Easter with. In Marseille, time stretches out indefinitely. She comes several times, that first morning. She holds my hand tight when I take her for a walk around all my favorite places, from the Vieille Charité center to the Malmousque rocks. She swims in her panties in the icy April water, with a smile all the way to her ears, and stiff nipples. On the last day she slaps me, a precise resounding slap that makes my head spin. She doesn't notice that we're on rue Consolat.

She and the child go out when I'm still asleep, they buy the first asparagus and the first strawberries. She says make a wish, my darling, when I pick up a strawberry to eat it. She has no idea that I wish this would all come to an end at last, her volatility, her tantrums, her mad excesses, her madness. She has no idea how desperately I need consolation.

72

To celebrate the first anniversary of her audacious gesture, of her admission that tore through the March air, she takes me on a trip to Venice. The night train is canceled. She says never mind, and books us two seats on a flight at the last minute. She can always find a solution. She sails over the swell of life with an energy that commands admiration. Life and the world have to work to suit her, to satisfy her all-powerful wishes. She's alive.

On the train home from Venice, between Grenoble and Paris, she locks the door to our compartment and undresses slowly, without a word. She offers herself to me, terrifyingly beautiful, with her thighs open to reveal her moist early-morning snatch, and the window curtain drawn to reveal the moist early-morning countryside spooling past in a fog of greens.

73

She likes reading novels to me, she plays the various characters, putting on different voices and gesticulating with her arms during their conversations. She hasn't mastered any sort of cooking in an oven, despite many attempts. She says going to the cimena, going to the pimming swool. She says squaw when she refers to her musical scores, where's that Brahms squaw, I've lost my squaw of the Beethoven 132, you haven't seen my Schubert squaw have you. She often loses things, finds them, misplaces them again.

She takes me to the Philharmonic Society to listen to Schubert sonatas, she slips her hand in mine when the emotion gets too much. She opens her eyes in the morning, stares at me intently and says we've got to end this, it's going to kill her. She takes me to the Théâtre de la

Ville to see a Pina Bausch performance, she claps furiously and hoots *bravo* at the dancers, up on her feet for a long time, shouting bravo, bravo! Next to her, I'm flushed red with a combination of shame and pride. At the cinema the lights come up and she's a strange sort of mirror, her face swollen with tears looking back at my face swollen with tears. She says our hearts beat to the same rhythm, she says this unison is incredible, this communion is incredible. She says no one would understand it, no one.

She calls me in the middle of the night. She's crying desperately, helplessly. She says that's enough. She doesn't hear me, on the other end, choked by my tears, suffocating, reeling with pain, every part of my body hurting because it's impossible to imagine life without her. She hits me and my cheek keeps the red outline of her fingers spread over my white skin for a long time. She says she'd rather we split up, but she's here within the hour holding the program for the next season at our favorite theater, she wants us to book tickets for lots of shows for the year ahead, she's making plans, she's as chirpy as a newly hatched chick.

74

She wants us to go to the cinema, she wants us to make love, then she wants us to fall asleep in each other's arms, she wants us to stop messaging and talking to each other for a few days, she wants us to eat Japanese, she wants us to go away to the country for a weekend to rest, she wants me to stop crying, she wants to go to a party without me, she wants to have no responsibilities, she wants to be footloose, she wants to be free.

75

July comes along like a boomerang. Paris is asphyxiating, there isn't a breath of air. She smiles when she unwraps the yellow leather bag I give her for her birthday. The same day she gives me a red rose plant, which dies in only a matter of days because the heat is too much for it. She surprises us, the child and me, by joining us on the Atlantic coast where we've gone for our holiday. She drives so quickly she's stopped by the police for speeding. She hides a present in my suitcase, a starry scarf, a scarry starf. She laughs uproariously, giggles at anything, she's a child, she's six and a half when she builds sandcastles for hours, when she makes a boat for my daughter out of beachcombings. She leaves, and life is dreary and deathly dull once more.

She and the quartet are played on France Musique, she's touched when I tell her over the phone that I knocked at every door in the village to beg someone to lend me a radio, that I looked for somewhere I'd get good reception and that I listened to them religiously, lying on the grass, in amongst the insects, with my ear glued to the radio.

76

She says no, I will never, do you hear me, never get on a merry-go-round ride thing like that, a ride that turns you upside down, makes your heart lurch and makes you want to throw up. She doesn't listen when I mutter a punning Max Jacob poem, the rides derided, the rides tried and tested, I've lost … what's died? … I cried, she's narked when I make fun of her, when I call her a wimp, she says okay fine, go on then, I'll come with you, she sits next to me in the pod and screams enough to rupture my eardrums when we start twirling in the hot dark night air. She's grinning like a child when we get off, she says she wants another go straightaway, she says again, again, again, she's a child, I'm in love with a child. She says it's magical, this funfair, she smiles at me next to a stand with garish neon lights flashing "No limits," she listens as I recite more of the poem for her, ride out your ride, outstride your stride.

"*Mon manège à moi*," my own merry-go-round, is a song composed by Norbert Glanzberg in 1958, with lyrics by Jean Constantin, who mistakenly worked on a piece of music that was to be part of the soundtrack for

Jacques Tati's film *Mon oncle* and was not intended to be a song. It went on to become one of Edith Piaf's greatest hits.

The song says: You make my head spin, I have my very own merry-go-round – you.

77

She's frightened because I come home drunk one evening when she's looked after my daughter for me, so drunk that my teeth are black from the wine, my lips stained brown. She doesn't understand that I'm exhausted by this life she's offering me, this life that goes far too quickly but to which she won't completely commit, exhausted by her instability, her uncertainty, her abandoning me and her tantrums, exhausted by her princessy whims.

She can't cope with anything anymore, she hates it when I'm tired, when I want to go to bed early, she wants us to talk all night, to make love endlessly. She says I've run out of love for you and the ground opens up beneath my feet. She waits for me outside my school, like she used to, with a bunch of daisies. She comes to a wedding with me and plays the violin for my friends. She laughs at my daughter's jokes. She gets annoyed with me, she beats my chest with her balled fists, she begs for it all to end, at last. She calls me and offers to take us to the seaside, she says pack your bags and I'll come and pick you up first thing. She kisses me as if for the first time at the motorway service station between Paris and Honfleur. It's all about Sarah, unpredictable, temperamental, disturbing, changeable and terrifying as a moth.

78

She smiles at me when the child falls asleep on her, dribbling over her breasts during *The Rite of Spring*, which the three of us have gone to together. She helps me make the child's Advent calendar, she's six and a half when she hides surprises, she's a child, I'm in love with a child. She makes an orange-flavored cake, chicken curry, a tagine with preserved lemons. She's thrilled to be celebrating Christmas with me for the first time. She tries on a dress in a shop, she drags me into the fitting room, closes the curtain behind her, makes love to me standing up against the mirror. She insults me in an overcrowded Métro, she says she can't take any more, that honestly, this needs to stop. She comes to the Turkish baths with me, she lets herself be washed and massaged in the haze of steam. She buys two kilos of clementines at once and gobbles half of them in the Métro on the way to Les Lilas. She dances the best part of the night at a birthday party we're invited to. She's alive.

She asks for more rum in her mojito in a bar in Saint-Germain-des-Prés. She puts on a completely different voice to say for God's sake I ordered a mojito and I've basically got minty lemonade, can you explain that. She pretends not to notice that I'm sitting there opposite her, flushed scarlet with shame. She winks at me when the waiter comes back with a glass full of alcohol. She clinks her glass against mine to drink to freebie highs. She says here's to you, my love. Then her face darkens. She wants to end this relationship, she's not joking this time, this is for real. She says I don't want to hear from you. She says I won't contact you. She drinks her mojito through the straw. She says you're stifling me. She watches me cry, her face hard and her arms crossed.

79

It's all about Sarah, her cruel, unfamiliar beauty, her austere bird-of-prey nose, her flinty eyes, her murderous, killer eyes, her snake eyes with their drooping lids.

80

She doesn't call me. She doesn't run after me in the street, in the corridors of the Métro. She doesn't write to me over the coming days, she doesn't say we should go to the theater, go to see the sea, visit a garden, drink tea, eat Japanese. She doesn't ask for my news, she doesn't ask for news of the child. She doesn't know that my whole body's burning, that my head is a permanent inferno, that I've never felt such a powerful, gnawing physical pain. She goes out of my life just as she came into it, with gusto. Victorious.

In the evenings I come home from school talking to myself under dark skies that are all blue and pink. I shake from missing Sarah. I spend my days crying, tears roll silently down my cheeks, then my neck, and come to die on my breasts. My eyes are puffy and my cheeks burn with salt. I go to see *Mamma Roma* at the cinema, in one of the cinemas we used to go to, I shiver with cold, my teeth chatter, I don't understand the film at all, not at all. I walk through Paris for ages, in the rain. I talk to myself, like a lost soul. I walk around Paris, a lot. I often run, for the bus, after pigeons, after her. I walk around the city. Did we trawl up and down it all that much, enough for every street corner to bring back a memory of you? Isn't there a single fucking façade, a single fucking café, a single fucking tune, a single fucking pedestrian crossing, a single fucking color in the sky, a single fucking cinema, a single fucking trend, a single fucking beggar that's not haunted by you, you witch? I take a night train to the fairy-tale house, the house where we danced the boogie-woogie. I go to Marseille, I take the bus to Malmousque, I howl at the steely rocks, I howl till my lungs are raw. I'd give anything to have her here with me, in her panties, swimming in the icy golden water. I do the rounds, hauling my carcass onto Marseille's buses, visiting my *Cité radieuse* – that's what they call it, the "radiant housing development." Radiant, yeah, right. Radiant, my ass. Up on the roof overlooking the whole city, my head spins when I think I could just jump because her silence is making me so demented. I lie down on my back on the roof of the Le Corbusier building and cry for a long time, to the astonishment of tourists who carefully step round my body, without a word, with an obsequious smile.

It's March. The first of March, the first of Mars, like the god, like the planet. March, Mars, Marseille, the city of healing, the city of resilience, the astral city. My body's burning, even without any sea water. All these scars, and this fire in my belly when I catch glimpses of you, and every night the images of you that I see gliding over the ceiling like comets, and the Maison du Fada building, which you would love, and my wanderings through the stench, which you would find moving. The light's right in my eyes, strong bright light, so white and so direct, almost acidic. The light on Mars pierces right through bone, pieces the skeleton back together again, patches up the soul. It's good knowing you share the same cosmos.

81

In another medical dictionary. *Latence*: after a physical trauma, the time that elapses between the event and the appearance of repetitive trauma syndrome. This apparently silent period is frequently typified by withdrawal, difficulty adapting, depressive states or, conversely, paradoxical euphoria. Usually lasting several weeks to several months, it can be very brief or can last for years.

82

A sudden realization at Marseille station. It's March, two years after the sparking match, the smell of sulfur and the admission offered up like a gift. It's March, it's several weeks since I've heard the sound of her voice. She said I don't want to hear from you, I won't contact you. She's exhausting but I'm dying without her. I can't do this, it's too hard. I hold my breath as the phone rings unanswered, once, twice, three times. And then she picks up. I hear her voice. She says hello. She says hello. She's alive. She sounds sad, a bit dejected, she's got her miserable voice on, the voice I know well, muted, clouded, stripped of all love and all nastiness. My heart constricts. It's suddenly rather cold on Platform 2 at Marseille station. There's a silence, a very long silence. I can hear her breathing and I wish I could swallow it. I look at my feet, and then at the sky. Over there, above the trains, there's a cloud sailing to join the other clouds.

She says I wanted to call you, you know, but I couldn't do it, because I need to tell you, I'm not well, it's serious, I've got breast cancer.

II

1

It's a spring almost like any other, a spring to depress the best of us. A weird spring, full of hot nights and cold rain. Here in this clammy room, I just can't take my eyes off her naked body and waxy scalp, her cadaverous profile. For one last time I study every part of her body, this body I love so much. I want to etch it into myself forever, her claw-like toes, the delicacy of her ankles, the touching curve of her calves, the softness of her thighs, her strange hairless snatch like a baby's, or an old woman's, her forgiving stomach. I want to etch into myself forever how beautiful her breasts are, both of them. I don't want to look at her face. I'm frightened of seeing her sleep. I'm frightened of seeing her die. I'm frightened of wanting to kiss her one last time. I'm frightened of waking her up. I'm frightened she'll come back to life.

Right now she's asleep, at last. She's dead.

I get up without a sound, in this dirty, gray dawn, this filthy dawn, I tiptoe out of the bedroom. My heart's beating furiously. I don't waste time dressing, I ram my clothes into my bag, put on my shoes and glance around this apartment where I've felt at home. I'm kept back for a moment by a burst of pink in the right-hand corner of the room. Magnolia flowers knocking against the windowpane, beautiful big magnolia flowers, their splayed petals full of dew and sunlight. I open the front door, close it behind me without a sound. I'm in my nightclothes in the light of a new day. I don't look around at the street but start to run, with all my might. I run like a madwoman through the streets of her suburb, this place I've ended up knowing by heart. I'm frightened she'll come after me, as she so often has, that she'll grab my sleeve to stop me, that it will all start again. I arrive at the Métro station out of breath and go down the steps four at a time, push through the metal gates with a nudge of my hips and throw myself into a carriage that sets off immediately, thank God. The Métro's taking me away. I'm far away already. I won't see her again. She's dead. I won't smell her smell again. She's dead. I won't stroke her body again, I won't make love to her again. She's dead. I won't watch, stunned, as her mouth tells me she doesn't love me anymore, she's no longer in love with me. I'm saved.

The Métro speeds through the darkness. I catch my breath. I swallow the taste of iron, of blood in my mouth. I run my hands over my face. My fingers still smell like her snatch. I sniff them like a lost soul. My love. My dead love. The smell, on my fingers, of my dead love's snatch.

So I must leave. Quickly. Not stay in this city. For two days, maybe three, I walk around Paris, a lot, almost nonstop. Night and day. I cross back and forth over the river. I often run. For the bus, after pigeons, after her. I walk around my city. Did we trawl up and down it all that much, enough for every street corner to bring back a memory of her. I must take a train, a plane. A boat. Get away. Quickly. I'm frightened I'll be found. They'll know what I've done. They'll flush me out. With death on my heels. She is death. Sarah is. I'm frightened she'll catch me in her nets again. I don't want to see her eyes anymore. Her beautiful, beautiful eyes. Her drooping eyes.

I try to breathe calmly, and think. I need to come up with a plan. A plan of action, a plan of attack. I need to deal with this. She's dead, for fuck's sake. She doesn't love me anymore. She doesn't want to love me anymore. She doesn't want any more of those mornings when the blaring radio can't begin to separate our two bodies, stunned by how much they love each other. She doesn't want any more laughing down the phone, or the pleasure of our words and our jokes being so well matched, or the way we're so perfectly in tune that life rings true the whole time. She doesn't want any more of our excursions, our getaways, our escapades. She doesn't want any more reunions that make our whole bodies quiver, our hands shake and our stomachs turn upside down. She's dead. I'm not sure. But I think she died, one spring night. A spring almost like any other, a spring to depress the best of us. And I was the one who killed her. I'm not sure. But I think I killed her. She said she didn't love me anymore. She had this cancer, of the breast, in her breast. Her breasts that I licked, while she smiled at me. She said my love, my love. And then afterward, straight afterward, she said she didn't love me anymore. And she died. Perhaps. I couldn't take my eyes off her naked body and her waxy scalp. Her corpse.

2

My little girl. My child who's so sweet and so funny. My living child who came out of my belly alive; what a wonder. My child who hasn't stopped living ever since, and still lives on. I'm going to have to leave her. I'm going to go. Without her. As far away as possible. To forget Sarah's profile in the disgusting light of early, early morning. Her ashen profile in the ashen light.

I'm going to run away to wash out my eyes. I'm breathing far too quickly. My whole body hurts. I know what I must do. My every move is sharp and precise, I heave myself onto the tips of my toes to rummage through the top of the cupboard. My hands grope blindly, eventually touch the strap, I pull, and my backpack thumps onto my head. My red backpack. I open it, zip, zip, the two zip fastenings. I pack a pair of jeans, a few T-shirts, some panties, a big scarf and a warm sweater. I get dressed. Another pair of jeans and another sweater. I don't take any skirts, I don't take any dresses and I don't take any blouses. I make my escape. With death on my heels. Is she awake now? Over there in her apartment with the magnolias? Is she amazed not to find me beside her? She must be wondering where I've gone, after that night spent curled against each other. Our bodies locked together. She might be thinking I've gone out to buy breakfast. That I'll be back. That I'll smile at her. Carrying a paper bag with two little *pains au chocolat*. A slightly greasy brown paper bag. Like every morning in the world after a night of lovemaking. And my fingers, which still smell like her snatch, gripping the paper bag. But no. She's dead. I know she is. She won't come back to life. She won't come back to her senses. She won't call me. She won't say she was wrong and she loves me and I must come back. She'll stay there, lying on her bed. The *dame aux magnolias*. I know it. And her body will be found at a time of day when the burst of pink from those flowers makes a shadow-puppet garland around her bald forehead.

A low-cost airline ticket. That's what I buy, clicking nervously on the first offer I find, not thinking, about anything. And this is something people dream of, buying a one-way ticket, a ticket to adventure, an idea that people nurture to keep themselves calm when life gets too complicated, too exhausting, the kids too noisy, anyway I'm getting out of here, I'm going a long way away and leaving it all, I'm going to catch a plane and never come back, start a new life somewhere else, and no one will know where, alone, and blissfully happy. I don't think, I just click, again and again, I validate, I say yes to every question the computer asks, yes, yes, yes, I don't have any choice, I have to go, I have to forget her cadaverous profile, her waxy scalp and the taste of blood in my mouth. The flight is very early the next morning, so early that I decide I need to go and sleep at the airport, so that's what I do, I leave, with my red backpack, I slam the door to my apartment, there's no knowing when I'll be back, in a few days, in a few weeks rather, yes, that's right, in a few weeks, when this has all settled down a bit, and I can breathe normally again, and the terrible images have dissolved among all the other terrible images I've seen, the seething mass of plastered-down fur on kittens drowned in the sink at the house in the country, the old woman knocked down by an HGV on the pedestrian crossing outside the post office, scenes of concentration camps being liberated seen in a room with drawn curtains one scorching hot day, the twin towers of 9/11 and people throwing themselves out of windows at the tops of the buildings, the hypnotic sight of Saddam Hussein's hanging, his great puppet-on-a-string body dislocated on the end of the rope.

I fall asleep quickly in the high-speed Métro. For several days now I've been walking around Paris so as not to be found, sheltering in bookshops to avoid the icy showers that contrast with the burning hot nights spent on the banks of the Seine, catnapping down by the water that fidgets as if locked in combat with some dark enemy. I fall asleep, lulled by the sway of this train cutting through unfamiliar suburbs, which all seem like possible sanctuaries because their names don't mean anything to me, La Courneuve, Le Blanc-Mesnil, Sevran-Beaudottes, Villepinte. When I get to the airport I immediately feel a little better. Almost reassured. She definitely won't come looking for me here. Her eyes won't catch up with me. Nor will her vampire smile. I won't be found here. I won't be told that she's dead. In her magnolia bath. That she never woke up. No one will ask me what I know, no one will interrogate me about her last night, about the taste of blood in my saliva, about my frantic escape. I disappear into the belly of this huge airport. I become one of those anonymous figures no one gives a damn about. At the duty-free shop I buy the components of a feast, to celebrate. Things I never eat. Huge bags of sweets. I try out several luxury-brand eye-shadows. I'm in no hurry.

I've become someone nobody knows. No one knows I'm here. No one talks to me. I look at bottles of spirits, their beautiful engraved boxes, I take the time to leaf through a guide to Italy. I'm almost thrilled to have this enforced holiday. I think about my little girl, about how I'll explain this to her when I come home. I've left her with her grandparents for now. I know she must be asleep, buried in her eiderdown, happy with this impro-vised arrangement. I'll tell her I went to Italy to heal a broken heart. It'll become one of those legendary stor-ies that's told again and again over coffee, sitting around the table after a family Sunday lunch. My little girl will think her mother really was like a character in a novel. I mean, there's a fictional glamour to it, run-ning away to heal your passion, abandoning your child for a while in order to allow your heart to scar. I stop for a moment at some neatly arranged bottles of per-fume. On a shelf I see the one Sarah wears. I pick it up, spritz it on my left wrist and bring it up to my nose. The pain is instant. My stomach lurches. I bite my fist to stop myself wailing. I run out of the shop, my plastic bag with the sweets in one hand and my scarf in the other. I run all the way to the window that looks out over the tarmac, until I can't go any further. It's dark outside. I come crashing up against the darkness. Orange lights flash on the runways. Huge airplanes stand there peacefully, placidly, waiting to be full of passengers. It's all so quiet. It's as if I suddenly can't hear anything anymore, as if a vast silence has just descended on the world. I collapse against the window. I feel as if I'm going to throw up but I start sobbing, stricken, prostrate, devastated.

3

It's a long night, filled with images of Sarah amid the constant teeming hubbub in the bowels of the airport, the sound of suitcases on wheels, of delays, announcements, people crying, people on the phone, caught between one life and another, in this suspended time when no one really knows where they are, what they're doing or why they're doing it. The fascination of being here, in the middle of the night, the fascination of being here, alive, in the middle of life, despite the deafening pain filling every part of me and the despair roaring deep inside me.

A nightmare. All the salesgirls in the airport's shops, all the air hostesses, all the female passengers are called Sarah. There is now only one woman's name – hers. I must be called Sarah too. I want to check my passport to see, I look for it, calmly at first then anxiously, turning out the pockets of my moleskin coat, nothing, the outside pockets of my backpack, nothing, I start to panic, you see I want to run away, to get on a plane and be done with all this, but without a passport I can't, for sure. People call out to each other and because every woman is called Sarah, it's total chaos, no one knows who's calling who, I hear her name everywhere, spoken by guys kissing women who are about to catch a flight, goodbye, Sarah, my love, shouted by fathers yelling at their children, and enunciated in public announcements over the loudspeakers. I go to the airport's police booth to tell them I've lost my passport. The policeman asks my name to register my case. I tell him. He starts laughing loudly and replies ominously but that's not possible, is it, only the Sarahs survived.

I'm curled up on some plastic chairs. I'm cold. And in pain. I miss her. The hell are you, bitch?

I get on the plane as the darkness starts to fray. I know there'll be daylight up above the clouds, what a relief. I don't look at my fellow adventurers, I don't really want to know who's with me on this journey. I'll be up in the sky soon, and that's just about all that matters to me. The great peaceful benevolent plane takes off. With my nose against the window I survey all the distance being put between her and me, and I feel like laughing. That's it, it's over. I'm saved. A miraculous survivor. The thought of my daughter cuts through me, I think of the life we both lead. When I pick her up from her school playground in the pretty evening light, her cheeks flushed from so much playing, the overwhelming happiness of watching her little legs accelerate when she sees me and feeling the impact of her body against mine. Our errands around Paris, our trips on the Métro, our outings on weekday evenings, even if it's not very sensible and she'll be tired the next day. I think she's rather like those between-the-wars children, those thousands of faces I studied in obscure old books, looking for God knows what, or maybe just God. The time we spend lying on the Moroccan rugs in her bedroom, telling each other things, listening while she tells me what it's like, what life's like, when you're nearly four, the fears that are already there in the pit of your stomach, the hopes you nurture, the dreams you whisper about and the pleasures you discover. Perhaps I should have let her father know, told him I'm going to Italy, that I'll be back in a while and – most important of all – ask him to take good care of her, explain that I need to sort some things out but I'll be back soon. It sounds a bit mafioso, putting it like that, and I'm not sure he'd understand. Silence is often better. He'll get the picture, anyway, when he realizes I'm not picking up my phone, and knocks at my door go unanswered.

Through the window I admire the outline of islands edged with sand, the European system of parceling up the land, truncated woods and bare soil, what looks like virgin soil, tended, yes, that's it, tended soil. The patterns left on the land by the backwash, like a never-ending conquest. The last shudders of this plane that, from a distance, must look like a bird washing itself in a rivulet of rainwater on a sunny day.

I've forgotten how much it can hurt your ears when the plane lands. But I take pleasure in every pain. My seized-up back, fine, my stiff neck, yes, my eardrums exploding, why not, every pain in my body means I momentarily forget the pain in my heart, the pain I have to live with now that she's dead, that she might be dead, the pain of having killed my love, of not being able to die instead of her. The fleeting splendour of the mountains around Lake Garda takes my breath away for a moment. So is this how it goes? Life can stop, love can die, and the world can keep going, right there, at the same time, in the same space, dazzlingly beautiful?

4

Rain pounds onto my burning cheeks and mingles with my scalding tears. I'm hot, so hot, as I wander, distraught, through these empty Milanese streets, and the raindrops really do me good, these heavy, late-April raindrops, I can almost hear them spatter individually as they strike the pavement, clattering like tap-dancing. The rain smells of oysters and tastes like *sake*, I'm aware of a huge gray cloud hovering just overhead, swollen with sea water, probably straight from the ocean. I left the airport at midday and I'm still running away, literally. If I weren't so tired I would actually be running. I dive down into a Metro station and my body decides for me, it chooses where to change, and I end up on the line that heads there, to where Isabella lives, I told her I'd be coming, it was an emergency, and I wouldn't stay.

There's no one in the Metro carriage, in fact there's no one anywhere, I wonder if it's still raining, I close my eyes for a minute. And the Metro suddenly accelerates up a hill, preparing to loom out of the dark confining tunnel, like a child emerging from its mother's insides, the carriage shudders more and more powerfully and there's a momentary suspense, perhaps just a second, and then it hurtles out, the sudden colors, the sudden noise, the sudden air. Sunlight floods the empty carriage, but it doesn't matter anymore, I'm so weak, huddled on my seat, I'm the baby expelled from the mother-city, I've got the same puffy face like a newborn boxer, the same ringing in my ears, the same urge to scream because breathing is difficult, and an explosion inside my head because … because a long time ago we used to get up on Sunday mornings to go and watch films at our favorite cinema. So early that when people were only just starting their Sunday routine we'd be catching the Métro home for something to eat, slightly groggy from spending two hours in darkness at the cinema when we were still half asleep. We would lie down at the end of the carriage, where there are six seats, two sets of three facing each other, and, lulled by the swaying and jolts in this other darkness, we waited for just one thing, the exact moment when the carriage tore itself from the ground to join the outside world. Lying on our backs, our eyes wide open, we waited for the sky, which appeared in a flash, and the intoxicating light that made our heads spin for a moment. And then, in her voice that I love so much, she would always say, look at that sun, my sweet.

5

For goodness' sake, I still can't get rid of this taste of blood. Assassin! I think I see on everyone's lips, even though they're Italian. Murderer! Lost cause! Killer hands! I killed her when she was already dying, in that pallid night air, I killed her because I couldn't bear to see her die, I couldn't bear to watch her lips open and say I don't love you anymore, I couldn't bear to see her suffer, to watch her suffer from an illness that I myself have buried in her breast, her left breast, where her heart is, an illness like a dagger to the heart, and me wielding the hand that holds the blade. I killed her because it was impossible for me to live with her, by her side, to be her partner, to travel this road together, I killed her because she loved music more, I killed her because I couldn't bear the sight of her emaciated body, her waxy scalp and her cadaverous profile. I killed her because she had tantrums like a diva. I killed her because I hated her, because I loved her so much I wanted to die instead of her.

Well, actually, I'm not sure. I don't really remember what happened. We made love. Almost the same as a crime, when it comes down to it. So maybe she isn't dead, maybe she's playing the violin, back there, in her house bathed in the pink light of magnolias. She's probably working on the octet. I remember that, I know how it goes.

6

Isabella comes quickly. I've been waiting only a few minutes on the square where she said she'd meet me, when she appears with a huge smile. She's wearing a pretty black dress, elegant suede boots and sunglasses that hold back her hair. Her cheeks are pink. She cries *ciao* when she sees me across the street and, just for a moment, I forget everything. She runs over and gives me a big hug, holding me to her tightly, a real *abbraccio*. She says have a good look at where we are, then you'll always find your way. This square is the Piazza della Conciliazione. What I hear is: consolation.

She lives very nearby, a large apartment all done in white, with old parquet flooring. She has a study with bookshelves right up to the ceiling, three cats that stalk proudly through the large rooms, a gorgeous kitchen with a huge wooden table that you instantly want to sit at, to have a coffee or write a few lines, and a balcony where you can read next to a deliciously sweet-smelling jasmine. I immediately feel at home, sheltered, safe, cut off from the world. No one will come looking for me here, that's for sure, and no one knows me here, I'm transparent, unknown, incognito. Innocent.

I don't know when I'll go back to Paris, I tell Isabella, I'd like to see a bit of your country, go a bit further than Milan, maybe all the way to Naples, catch night trains because I don't have any money and because I really love them, yes, why not all the way to Naples, I'd like to wake up by the sea in a city that glitters and stinks as much as Marseille, that's how I imagine Naples, is that right, Naples stinks, doesn't it? And that's what I need, I think but don't actually tell her, I need stench to smother the smell of blood that won't leave me, following me like a reddened cloud loaded with bloodied sea spray, the smell I find everywhere, I'm steeped in it and it writes the word *assassin* on my forehead. Napoli, she asks and howls with laughter, that great raucous laugh of hers, but it's the ends of the earth, *carina*, Napoli's in the south, it's almost another country, you know, another life. Well, there you are, I mumble, that's what I want, another life.

7

I remember that, life suspended, this life put on pause, when I held my breath, weightless, waiting. Yes, I was waiting. I floated through the passing days, I floated and tried to pretend everything was normal. I woke up feeling sick and was tired in the middle of the day, with an impossible, sledgehammer tiredness, as if I was the one who'd gone to Japan. I tried to tell her about it on Skype, where we exchanged a few words at ridiculous times of day and night. Talking in unison, we counted the days till she'd be home. Only eighteen more days. Still eighteen days to go. I focused on her mouth, on the screen, as if my life depended on it. Her lips articulated loving words that reached me with a slight delay. When we were about to hang up, the Japanese earth started to shake appallingly and it was like contagious seasickness, it felt as if my room was moving too, my floorboards were juddering, my body was flickering. We kept up our banter from our respective beds all through the earthquake, and I couldn't help thinking that we were the earthquake, that our relationship was the seismic shift that made everything judder for several kilometers around, that it was a convulsion, a cataclysm.

A catastrophe. I remember that, thinking believe me, no one will come out of this unscathed.

8

I collapse on the sofa in Isabella's study and cover myself with some Indian fabric lying nearby. I plunge into instant sleep, like fainting. From this comatose state, I can hear Isabella do some housework, have a shower, go out for something, clack-bam the door of the apartment, come back in typing on her phone, clack-bam the door of the apartment, talk to her cats in Italian, bash things around in the kitchen, make something to eat, swear and grumble out loud. I wish I could stay here my whole life, sleeping to the sound of people getting on with their lives, people who don't know, the naïve sound of people who've done no wrong.

When I wake up, I peel two kilos of potatoes, to help her, without a sound and without a word. The radio chatters in Italian next to us, the cats doze. I wonder vaguely what my daughter's father will say when he realizes I've vanished. He's such a lightweight I'm not even sure he'll raise the alarm. I feel as if I'm in cotton wool, in a life that's been stopped, someone else's life, someone who's not me. Isabella thinks I'm very pale, says I should get some fresh air. She tells me how to get to the Milan Triennale at the Palazzo dell'Arte in

Sempione Park. I have a feeling that if I don't take her advice, if I don't leave straightaway, then I'll never set foot outside her apartment again, I'll stay cloistered and prostrate in this unfamiliar apartment in this unfamiliar city. I don't take anything, just put on my moleskin coat and go out, clack-bam.

The streets in this neighborhood are wide, lined with big houses that are far more than houses, they're villas, antique residences. On Via XX Settembre the pavements are overrun with gloomy mauve wisteria. I eye the huge buildings as I walk along, their columns, their dark contemptuous shutters. I think about Roman wealth, the notion I have of decadent, exhilarating Roman wealth. I walk under a delirious sun, a shameless, indecent sun. An impossible sun, a sun I don't deserve. The Palazzo dell'Arte is sumptuous, its gardens magnificent. All this beauty smacks me in the face, hurts me, gets under my skin like a penknife. I want the whole world to be tainted like my bloodstained hands, the sky to be low and gray, and the sun to turn its face away just like me, ashamed and guilty.

When I get back to Isabella's apartment, the table over by the window is laid, old cutlery and beautiful cut-crystal glasses are artfully arranged on a large white linen tablecloth, and the room is lit by candles. She laughs at my astonished expression, she must think I'm surprised and glad that she's treating me like this, she says I've invited some friends for dinner with us, she doesn't know that all this pomp is what's making me gawp moronically, that I think it's opulent and grotesque, that it only needs a few bunches of grapes for us to be right there with the stale old Romans, and that all her grand preparations make me feel sick. I also feel sick when I see the beautiful evening dress she puts on and comes mincing over to show me, also sick at her heavily madeup face, and sick again when I hear the guests ring the doorbell.

I make an effort, in spite of everything, I brush my hair, put a bit of blusher on my cheeks. In the mirror I try to smooth my hair, and to look a bit more cheerful. Waste of time.

9

I'm grateful to the woman who introduces herself to me with a simple *ciao, sono Benedetta*, for not trying to make conversation with me as she starts to make a lemon sauce for the pasta, and for letting me help her. I'm like a puppet, copying her every move, I crush a clove of garlic and blend it with the lemon juice she squeezes, I add olive oil and Parmesan, and blend and blend and blend. I watch, hypnotized, as the different ingredients amalgamate to form a cream, it's as if I've never cooked before. The other guests arrive. Isabella tells us where we're sitting, everyone sits down, an expensive-looking bottle of wine is uncorked, an incredible wine, a classic even, one of the guests seems to say after tasting it, a man with dark hair and a boorish look about him. There are eight of us. I don't understand much of what they're saying, everyone talks very loudly and very quickly, with lots of gesticulating and laughter, I catch only occasional words that are similar to the French and give me an idea of the content of the conversation. It doesn't bother me, anyway, I'm here but not really, I'm in the bedroom in the apartment in Les Lilas, next to Sarah's sleeping body, next to Sarah's dead body, next to her skin that's still warm for a while yet, next to her beautiful impassive face, next to her bald waxy scalp wreathed with the shadow of the magnolias. Lilacs and magnolias, a beautiful bouquet for a dead woman. Well, you deserve it, my love.

I can't eat a single morsel of the meat Isabella serves as the *secondi piatti*, I see Sarah's body in it, Sarah's body dismembered and cut up next to the mashed potato made with the potatoes I peeled myself. I look at them one after another, all of them, the seven other people around the table, in their beautiful clothes, with their beautiful words in their beautiful language and their beautiful gesticulations, and they're ogres devouring her body, tearing her flesh with their teeth, not leaving so much as a scrap. It makes me retch. There's pink-grapefruit sorbet for dessert, I accept it with pleasure, the chill and sourness run down my throat and quell my need to be sick. I take myself off to bed unceremoniously when the guests are still here. I go out like a light again, as if fainting, to the sound of their gluttons' voices and their cannibals' laughter.

10

I remember that, I know how it goes. Early mornings next to her. Four minutes past seven, the radio blaring news about Syria in the clammy bedroom, I want to bury myself in sleep that's broken and already lost, in the slightly tepid sleep that comes after nights of voracious lovemaking, nights of ravenous, all-consuming, insatiable lovemaking, those nights of lovemaking when I get the feeling we won't survive, we'll die here, like this, those nights of lovemaking when we eat each other's hearts, yes, that's it, we eat each other's hearts crushed into little crumbs in the palms of our hands, and when I cry inside because I so want to be subsumed, to melt, to drown and disappear into her body. I remember that, I know how it goes, those feral evenings spent pacing the city. Thirty-four minutes past midnight, in the Parisian night, and we intrigue people. They turn silently to study our slightly unsteady silhouettes that never let go of each other, our faces both glowing with

the same strange expression, full of pleasure, impu-
dence, poise and nerve, an edge of insolence, too, yes
surely, the impertinence deep in our eyes. In the taxi
home we add up everything we've had to drink, and
the inventory's never enough to explain our thrilling
intoxication. It's because our drunkenness is down to
the hours we've spent together, to the way we throw
ourselves into this mad life, to the time stolen from time
itself. I remember that. As soon as we're together, the
magic begins.

11

I wake late, exhausted, as if I've been running all night.
Isabella has been up for a long time, she's chatting happily with two of last night's guests in the kitchen. The
dark-haired man, who still looks just as boorish and who
has an incredibly deep voice, and a woman of about
forty with wavy gray hair, looking very elegant in a silk
negligee and whose name, I remember, is Lisa. I gather
that they're a couple. Isabella tells me they don't live in
Milan, they've come for the weekend and slept in the
spare room, they'll be leaving at the end of the afternoon, heading back to Slovenia where they live. She
sends me off to have a shower. I stay under the luke-
warm water for a long time, sitting in the bath with the
shower head between my thighs. I think of all the times

we made love, Sarah and I, and I wonder who'll touch my body now that I won't be seeing her anymore, now that she doesn't love me anymore, she doesn't want me anymore, she chose to die instead.

The conversation in the kitchen is in full swing. I'm relieved I don't understand all of it, as I can listen to it like listening to a lullaby, not paying any attention to the words but enjoying the melody. Isabella puts a lot of cream in the coffee she pours me, hands me a pretty plate with a big slice of *pinza*, a speciality from Trieste brought by her guests, a sort of brioche that James Joyce used to love. On the little card that comes with it: *conserva nella sua confezione originale ad una temperatura non inferiore ai 15°C*, then *da consumarsi preferibilmente entro il* and it doesn't say a date. I wonder what temperature Sarah's body would have to be kept at to stop it rotting.

I ask about Trieste, Joyce's city, a place I know nothing about. Lisa is unstoppable, she starts talking very quickly in a combination of Italian, English and French, and I gather that her grandfather grew up in Trieste and she spent all her holidays there as a child, that she doesn't go back much, but every time she does it's very emotional. When her grandfather died she inherited his apartment but she doesn't have time to look after it, it's falling into disrepair. They live in Slovenia now, she and the dark-haired man with the deep voice. Trieste was on their way to Milan, they stopped off for a night, they slept in her grandfather's apartment and, first thing in the morning, they dropped in to buy a *pinza* at the patisserie where Joyce used to buy his.

With its seven centuries of history, Sforza Castle is an extraordinary record of Milan's glory days but also of times of crisis. It is now one of the most significant monuments in the city and in all of Lombardy, dear to the locals and known to tourists the world over: it's not only a spectacular building, but also a valuable setting for many genuine masterpieces and a place of study.

Isabella insists on taking me to see the castle. When we stop briefly at a café, we talk about love and the agonies you have to experience in order to appreciate the joys. She doesn't ask any questions when I start to cry silently. She just says – gently, in her irresistible accent – you have to get through the nights and be fulfilled during the day. And then she goes off to work and leaves me there, at the foot of those ancient stones.

I drag my feet through the gravel around the castle. I go into the museum without much conviction, my cheeks clouded with salt. I stammer as I ask my way. I'm looking for the room painted by Leonardo da Vinci. At the shop I buy a postcard to send to Sarah, and I write it straightaway, standing there next to the mugs and fridge magnets featuring *The Last Supper*. Then I try to go back to Isabella's apartment. I get lost. It's Sunday, in Milan and everywhere else. Everything's closed. There's wisteria everywhere.

12

When I get back to the apartment Lisa and the man with the deep voice are packing their bags. Using a mixture of languages, Lisa asks me if I'd like to visit Trieste, whether I'd be interested in using her grandfather's apartment for a few days. If I am, I'll need to pack too because it's a long drive to Slovenia and they want to get there before nightfall.

I open my red backpack, zip-zip, stuff in my scarf and the sweater I'd taken out, close it up, zip-zip, run to kiss Isabella and almost scream at Lisa I'm ready, all done, with a peculiar cheerfulness in my voice. All at once, real joy scoops me up. I stop thinking about Sarah, stop thinking about her emaciated body that I left when I ran away, stop thinking about my child, my child's father, my parents, my students, all I think about is this car I'm about to get into, this unfamiliar car driven by unfamiliar people who are going to take me to an unfamiliar city. I feel light, I could laugh out loud. It's like euphoria, the end of an adventure, the blissful moment when the world stops spinning at last.

13

I remember this, the violence between us, Sarah's furious green eyes, but no, not green, her absinthe-colored eyes with the drooping lids, her spiteful mouth, her wild gesticulations. I know how it goes. I leave. I run away. I'm already running away. I take the Métro. And then here I am, always Saint-Lazare station, suburban trains, it doesn't matter which, the first available. And, just for a moment, it's fine, yes, everything's fine. There's the swaying, like a reprieve. I stop any-old-where, a place chosen at random, and step slowly off the train. I remember this. It's August, the girls are all golden brown under their light summer dresses, the boys in Bermuda shorts smell of hair that's spent too long in the sun. I don't go far, ever, I'm happy to stop at the first café I find. Often the Station Café, sometimes the Travelers' Café. I don't really care about the name, I always order the same thing, anyway: a lemonade. I know how it goes, the bubbles tickling my nose when I'm burning all over with misery, the lemon taste projecting me into childhood, or at least somewhere where *everything's fine.* I wait there for a long time, stroking the condensation that's settled on my bottle until it beads into water. My mind is blank. I watch passersby, envying them for living in the perfect ignorance they seem to evince. Maybe I'm also slightly contemptuous of them. Poor bastards. Poor bitches. You don't know. How long the pain lasts.

14

I fall asleep quickly in the car, lulled by Lisa and her partner's conversations in Italian and Slovenian. They spend the whole time raising their voices, as if constantly arguing, but they call each other *amore*. A long time later we stop on the motorway. The dark-haired man, who doesn't speak a word of French, offers me a coffee with infinite gentleness, almost pity, in his eyes, as if he knows what I'm doing, as if he gets it, all of it. It's an isolated moment, suspended in time, nothing happens, his brown eyes are just suddenly there looking at me, in all the bustle of the service station, brown eyes that look at me unblinking for a good while. He nods as he passes me a paper cup. I feel as if I've been rumbled. When we get back into the car he hands over the driving to Lisa and asks me to sit in the front, next to her. He lies full length on the backseat, and I find it very touching seeing him like that, his great bulky body stretched out like a child's on those uncomfortable seats. As soon as we're back on the motorway he starts to snore.

Lisa and I talk in a strange pidgin language. She tells me about her relationship with the Slovenian bear, how they met when they were very young one snowy day just before Christmas, in his country, where she'd gone to visit a girlfriend. She describes their long life together, the life they lived like children and then the vagaries of fate that meant they couldn't have any, their happiness for all that, particularly since they moved out of the city to a small house in the countryside.

I doze for a while, dumbstruck by the glorious evening light, light skimming across landscapes of vineyards that I watch roll by hypnotically. As we drive past Venice the radio plays "Hit the Road Jack" and Lisa joins in with Ray Charles for the chorus, hit the road, Jack, and don't you come back no more, no more, no more, no more.

15

We reach Trieste as the sun sets. At a turn in the road, around a bend, all at once, there, offered, like a gift, spread out as it has been for years, glimmering gold, blindingly beautiful, the Adriatic. The sight of it is like a punch to my heart. How can there possibly still be beauty after the catastrophe, after the unspeakable? How can these things go on in a life without her? The sea so resplendent, the soothing warm air running through our hair, the tunes on the radio, a car on Italy's roads and this setting sun in a red that doesn't exist. An impossible sun.

Lisa and the Slovenian bear lead me through Trieste's narrow streets. Lisa warns me that her grandfather's apartment is in a terrible state, that she's really sorry she can't offer me anything better, she says she hopes I'll enjoy being here anyway, that it makes her happy to think someone will be living within these walls for a few days. The apartment is on the top floor of an old building. It hasn't been lived in for a long time. Lisa opens the door and the musty smell jumps out at me. She tells me nothing's changed here for fifty years, give or take, that no one's ever touched anything since her grandfather died, and he'd been living with the same decor for years. She shows me where I can find clean sheets, and how to open the door onto the terrace, gives me her phone number, tells me not to think twice before calling her if I need anything, and then they kiss me and leave, it's still a long way to Slovenia.

Silence. The first true silence since I ran out of the apartment in Les Lilas. A blank. I'm standing in the main room. Groggy. Silence. Silence. Silence. She's dead. I killed her. Her illness killed her. Our love killed her. She committed suicide. She took too high a dose of medicine. I killed her because I couldn't bear to see her suffer. I killed her because it was impossible, her mauled, emaciated body, her bald scalp. I killed her because she was driving me mad. I killed her because she didn't want to love me anymore. I don't know now. A blank, in my mind. I don't remember what happened. We made love, that, yes. And then. Is she really dead, even? I don't know now. I've forgotten everything.

16

I lock the door behind them. And all of a sudden it's party time. I'm a child who's been left home alone for the first time. I almost run over to throw open the door to the terrace. When Lisa showed me around the apartment I didn't appreciate that there was such a big terrace with a large table and a breathtaking view over the city and the sea. I can't get over it. I feel like dancing, singing, screaming at the top of my lungs. I open my red backpack, zip-zip, feverishly unpack my things and settle in. My few clothes tidily put away on hangers, my beauty products in a drawer in a bathroom cabinet. I take out my mobile, which I switched off the minute I ran away from Sarah's apartment. Just for a moment I feel like turning it on, to see whether she's called, or texted. I think she might be worried, that her voice might be in my voicemail, her voice that I love so much, her voice saying that she was wrong and she loves me and I must come back. And then I remember she's dead. I stuff the phone into an undercounter cupboard in the kitchen, in the bottom of a saucepan, along with its charger. I put another pan on top of the first one and close the cupboard.

I smooth out my clothes with the flat of my hand, put a bit of blusher on my cheeks, apply some mascara. The only thing I take with me is my purse. I'm already drunk on this sudden freedom, but I definitely intend to toast this, to celebrate it. In the mirror in the lift, which is as ancient as the grandfather's apartment, I wink at my reflection and whisper to the girl in the mirror, we're not doing too badly, are we, for a murderer.

Once outside, I feel like dancing. I just can't believe I'm here, alone, in this city I've never heard anything about, in the mild air of a late-April night. I saunter happily down the road, which is dizzyingly steep. Night has settled over Trieste. When I catch sight of the sea, it twinkles with the orange lights on boats. I save the pleasure of seeing it close up for tomorrow. I step into a chic-looking café, the Caffè San Marco, which – to my absolute delight – is also a bookshop. It turns out they serve food until midnight. Perfect, it's all perfect. I order *gnocchi al ragù* and a large bottle of sparkling water. The plate of food that's brought to me seems the most cheering thing in the world. I gobble down my food, laughing contentedly. The water bottle's so pretty that I shamelessly slip it into my bag, planning to use it as a vase in the apartment. When I get back, I run myself a bath. It's party time! I'm out of reach here, out of reach of the world. Nothing can happen to me. I settle for the night with a big smile on my lips, in the sofa bed Lisa told me to use. They have a bed made up with their sheets in her grandfather's old room, for when they stop off here between Milan and Slovenia, and she'd rather I didn't sleep in it. She didn't even show me that room and, unbelievably good girl that I am, I haven't so much as felt like opening the door. I fall straight into a deep sleep.

17

First light is barely appearing over Trieste when I open my eyes. I race out onto the terrace to check I wasn't dreaming and this place really exists. Yes, the incredible view's still there, even more beautiful in the dawn light. The roofs of houses spread as far as the eye can see and seem to dive off into the sea dancing in the distance, so blue, almost violet. In the old-fashioned kitchen I make myself some breakfast with what I find in the cupboard, some rice crackers and a bit of jam. I spot a bottle of grapefruit juice in a corner, check the best-before date and drink a great slug of it straight from the bottle, standing barefoot on the battered tiles. The acidity burns my throat, numbs my mouth and does me the power of good. I rummage through the drawers till I find a tiny strainer to make tea. I feel like Robinson Crusoe in this apartment, a sort of stowaway in the great ship of this building, on the great sea of the city. I search further afield, for some paper, rifling like a burglar through the drawers of a wooden desk, and I come across a wad of old paper. I go over to my red backpack, zip-zip, for a pen, then back out onto the terrace, barefoot, facing the unbelievable view. Seagulls perched on the brick chimneys all around me eye me contemptuously. I sit at the table on the terrace and tell myself I must write, to stop talking to myself inside my head, to try to remember what happened that night at Les Lilas. We made love, I know. But after that.

I spend a little time folding away the sofa bed and tidying the living room, I plump up a few cushions, raising clouds of dust. Without even thinking, I embark on a spring clean with whatever comes to hand. I shake all the cushions out on the terrace, the dust stinging my eyes and making me cough terribly, and I run a damp cloth over the shelves. In the kitchen I inventory all the utensils, I take the ones I like best out of their drawers and cupboards and line them up in a scrupulous row on the Formica table. I make the arbitrary decision to use these alone. A pretty blue metal teapot, an old kettle, a tiny wooden chopping board, cutlery that reminds me of my mother, and a salad bowl with flowers on it. I wash and dry them, then put them away in a cupboard, which I decree will be mine.

On a whim, I open the door to Lisa's grandfather's bedroom and stand there dumbstruck. It's an enormous room in comparison to the rest of the apartment, with beautiful parquet flooring and an extraordinary window, unlike anything I've ever seen, a huge circular window. I'm amazed to discover a bed quilted with toile de Jouy fabric, floor-to-ceiling cupboards with the same quilted covering in the exact same fabric. The whole effect is mind-blowing, like a pink and cream cocoon – slightly kitsch but also rather touching. It's disconcerting, jarring even, trying to picture an old man in this Marie Antoinette–style setting. I close the door very gently, as if not wanting to disturb something, and tiptoe away.

I try to get my things organized in the bathroom. I regret not bringing more clothes, more makeup, some jewelry. I'm thrilled when I find a music system in the small living room, and a few records next to it. I pick up the closest one. Schubert. My heart goes wild, I think of Sarah and my hands are instantly clammy and a ball forms in my stomach, I almost drop the record when my eyes alight on the words *first violin* and *second violin*, my heartbeat accelerates, I turn the record over, thinking this can't be possible, it really can't be a record by her string quartet, I hurt all over. *The Trout*, it says, and I laugh with relief. I promise myself I'll listen to the quintet when I get back from my walk. Strings and piano. There, nothing to do with Sarah at all.

18

A feeling of joy washes over me again when I step out of the apartment, lock up my haven, my hideaway, and slip into the lift, which creaks like an old man. It's going to be a beautiful day, the sky is absolutely cloudless. There's a sweet smell in the air that I don't recognize. I go down the street toward the city center, as I did yesterday evening, I walk past Caffè San Marco without stopping, despite the painted wicker chairs giving me the eye from the terrace. I want to see the sea, it's become an irrepressible urge, I want to know if it's the sort of sea you can swim in, if it's the sort of sea I could drown myself in, should the fancy take me.

I remember this, wandering around Marseille when she'd said I don't love you anymore, it's over, do you understand, it's over, I-don't-love-you-a-ny-more, clearly chopping up the syllables, I remember lying down on the roof of the *Cité radieuse* to howl my pain, radiant city, my arse, nothing radiant about anything, walking all the way to Malmousque chasing memories of us, going to have couscous with the old Jewish man who always calls me my girl, go ahead and eat, my girl, he said, handing me a plate, but I couldn't eat a thing, I put a ten-euro note on the table and scuttled away like a thief. I remember this, Marseille Saint-Charles station, words already jostling to get out of my mouth, the things I was so desperate to say to her, to say to her in a slow, clearly enunciated voice, the sort of voice you use to talk to someone who's ill, to someone who's out of their mind, come on, my love, we love each other, you know we do, don't you, and I remember her being one step ahead of me with what she had to say, with her words, terrible words I wasn't expecting, her murmuring, in her sad voice, I wanted to call you, you know, but I couldn't do it, because I need to tell you, I'm not well, it's serious, I've got breast cancer. I remember that, the chill in my body and that cloud going to join the other clouds, further away, above the railway tracks.

I don't understand this city at all, as I walk along I look at the architecture in the streets and nothing looks like anything else, it's all a bit bonkers but also nice and orderly, a city to make your head spin but that tries to trick you, I feel like I'm in Germany, Austria, France, even Sweden sometimes, here in Italy. What comes out of people's mouths is like this too, a layering, a mixture of languages and it's hard to tell who's who.

There among the multicolored façades the feeling of joy doesn't leave me, though. The sun bounces off everything, channeling down all the streets. And the sea, well, the sea's always there at the end of every street, the arrival point whichever route you take, every road is a one-way street to its salty smell. I try on dresses in a slightly kitsch shop, I nearly let myself be tempted by a green one before realizing I want it because it's almost the color of Sarah's eyes, I put it back on the rack in disgust and make my escape from the shop, *arrivederci*, and there you go. I stand outside a church for many a long minute, listening to a beautiful boy playing Viennese waltzes on the violin, I think how she wouldn't like this, she'd probably say he plays badly, that he's massacring the music by doing this, I know that if she were here she'd irritate me, she'd ruin my enjoyment, I reply inside my head, I do all the dialogue myself and play out the whole argument but it doesn't have much appeal. Life's crap without you here to answer back. What were you thinking, letting me kill you.

I order a latte at the Caffè degli Specchi, I think I'll have to buy myself at least one pair of sunglasses, I pay and set off on a long walk along the sea front. In a super-market I buy a 250-gram packet of *taralli* in olive oil and a bottle of *frizzante* water because it's getting very hot. I eat all the little snack biscuits straightaway as I walk on and on.

Everything's muddled up. Architecture, streets, buildings, languages, faces. I can't remember why I'm here, why I'm walking along the sea front in this city I don't know. The feeling of joy leaves in the same way it came, in a flash, abruptly, with no warning. There are signs on all the restaurants saying *ristorante chiuso* and I hear choose, the word bullies me, choose, choose, choose. I talk to Sarah as if she were here next to me. At the end of a street there are some beautiful red and white posters that persuade me to keep going, even though I'm suddenly tired and my feet have had it. I walk over softly, with slow hesitant footsteps. Are you coming, let's see what it says on those posters over there. Come on, my love. Come on, let's go. It says *vota Trieste, territorio libero di Trieste*, I think it must be about some elections and I'm reassured to see that my brain's still sort of working, despite the dark cloud that's just closed in around my head.

19

Beyond the posters there's a street that drops down gently toward an abandoned-looking building. It's so hot now. I've finished my bottle of sparkling water. I've been walking aimlessly since I left the apartment. As I get closer to the premises I realize this is a decommissioned naval port. There's no one here but it feels as if the place was left in a hurry, like a ghost town. The buildings are crumbling in places, their frameworks dismembered. There's a small blue house, which must have been somewhere for the workers to rest, and a couple of sheet-metal hangars that are still just about standing. The whole area is overrun with weeds, wild vegetation climbing anywhere it can. Stinging nettles lash at my ankles, shaking me out of my lethargy a little. I notice that I'm talking to myself, out loud, as if she's with me. I need to focus my mind again, remember what happened that night, in her apartment in Les Lilas, remember her dead woman's body and what she died of. I need to concentrate, to remember why I'm here, in Trieste, in Italy. It's important.

In between the hangars there's a pale-blue bench, a bench made of rough-hewn planks and with the paint slapped on carelessly. I wonder who did this, who took the time, here in this former naval dockyard, to make a small pale-blue bench. A workman during his lunch break so he could enjoy the sun for a while, drink a coffee with his workmates sitting on something other than the gravel on the ground, to lie down on, perhaps, just long enough for a tiny siesta. The place is deserted. There isn't a breath of air, not a whisper of shade. I collapse onto the little pale-blue bench. I hurt all over, in every part of my body. My mind's rambling. You can only just see the sea from here, but what you can do is hear it sing, calm and reassuring in the distance. It feels good picturing it close by, knowing it's there. I close my eyes.

I turn my face toward the light. Outside, I'm outside. A smell of smoke hangs in the air. Being here feels like returning from childhood. The white April sun beside the Adriatic is like the white April sun from when I was five years old. The scrappy garages made of a few pieces of wood and a lot of corrugated iron, the brick wall at the far end and the divided-up old garden at the foot of the blue house, it's as if I've been here before, it's as if I already know all this by heart. The almond green of tattered shutters on an old building, the smell of smoke that's going to my head, the birdsong. It's springtime, it's springtime, a spring to depress the best of us. I don't know why I came here, to this clapped-out Italy. Paris–Trieste, to forget her, forget Sarah? To go somewhere she's never been, to go to a place whose name she's never uttered? Virgin territory of her, of us. And here I am stumbling across childhood. The search for lost time is satisfied in Trieste.

I remember this, the car going like the clappers on the *périphérique* ring road, zigzagging as it weaves through the traffic. At red lights we look into each other's eyes, we can't help ourselves. The Sunday at Versailles we spent walking along *allées royales* paths, seeing red buds open on the perfectly pruned trees. The afternoons at her apartment, back in Les Lilas, drinking tea, coffee, then tea again, listening to music that makes her sing. The freedom of Wednesdays, without the child. How funny we found it; *it is great, though*. It is great – comma – though. The kisses, sometimes, sometimes not. One evening, she spends a long time trying to remember the name of a mathematical method she's just used. She can't remember it, she thinks hard, drums her fingers on the table, jumps to her feet to go and look it up on the Internet, but turns back straightaway. And, leaning against the doorframe, she says oh yes, that's it, I've got it, it's remarkable identities.

20

Stop laughing, please. Stop laughing inside my head, stop laughing next to me. Leave me, can't you? I killed you because I loved you, because I couldn't bear to watch you suffer any longer, to see your body, your gorgeous body, your queen's body, your body I so loved and so longed for, I couldn't bear to see it being fucked up by the illness. I told you all this, that evening. Just before. You know, do you remember? We made love. *I* remember. I know how it goes. My fingers deep inside you, deep inside a you who can hardly move anymore. My mouth on your dry lips. My kisses on your mauve eyelids. My wanting to make you come one last time. I'd already reached my decision at that point. I wanted you to come and then go to sleep, there, right there, in your house in Les Lilas. I wanted you never to wake up.

I remember that, I know how it goes. The kisses on rue Gracieuse. The kisses on rue Gracieuse, in the hidden little recess, our first kisses. She says it's like we're having an illicit affair. Cold hands, hers, and mine, red noses, hers, and mine. It's the first winter, the winter of that admission like a gift. The little packets of tissues bought the day before on rue Monge. I say we're like an old couple, doing our shopping together like this. The kisses on rue Gracieuse, they're kisses goodbye, aren't they, okay, because it can't go on, it's not possible, I have a partner, a child, a well-ordered life. And then, a few hours later, no, not okay. And who cares if life's weird, who cares if we've lost track of where we are, the Left Bank the Right Bank – who cares, who cares if we cross the Seine as if stepping over a gutter, who cares if we're both sometimes gloomy, often depressed. But there are the messages saying if we see each other this evening, you're not allowed to be a pain in the arse, the likes and dislikes in common, the epiphany cake bought to celebrate nothing in particular, the euphoria steadily taking hold of us over one of our first lunches, have they put something in the wine or what, and then, straight afterward, no that's not it, we're just good together. Winter padding by with muffled footsteps, watching the snow fall. I wonder whether she's noticed how much I've changed since she gifted me that admission with its struck-match smell, whether she knows me well enough to. Probably not. But here I am helping her choose glasses in all the shops in her neighborhood, and there she goes sending me suggestions for pieces of music to listen to, depending on my mood. The entry code to her building, the name of her perfume, the new tea I haven't heard of, the bookshops we've been into, the cafés we've come out of, and her hand mussing my hair.

I've found my way back to the apartment perched at the top of town. I've walked a long way, taking my time, looking carefully at each crossroads so I don't forget the route to the disused naval yard, to the little pale-blue bench that afforded me a few minutes' peace. Before going up, I stop off at the supermarket to get some things, to buy some provisions. The brand is written on all the products – Spar. I don't know what to buy, I don't feel like anything, but I am starting to get really hungry. I eventually take a basket, fill it up mindlessly. Spar, spar, spar. Oh yes, duel, joust, box, fight, fight, fight. My heart's thudding far too hard in my chest, reverberating up to my temples. I'm shaking all over, panicking. When I get to the yogurts I dissolve into tears. I see Sarah, as if it was yesterday, at the Korean restaurant, telling me she can't choose, that it's a problem, in life. That she wants everything and nothing. I don't know what to buy, I see fight, fight, fight everywhere, absolutely everywhere. I grab two packs of blueberry yogurts, my favorite, gnocchi with spinach, also my favorite, I only buy things I like, I think of those prisoners over in the States who get to have their favorite meal before being executed. The last days of a condemned woman.

I'm breathing heavily as I come back out of Spar with my bags of shopping, I try to fight back my tears and the irrational panic that gripped me in the supermarket. I must focus, I must. Life without her *is* still life. There's the little pale-blue bench, the smell of the sea. And after all, there is the child waiting for me back there. But love is betrayal. Love is betrayal, and I just can't do that. I'm unfailingly loyal. I don't know how to betray you, my love. I can't love again, do you know that? I hope I'll always remember the second just before I knew you existed, before I knew what would happen to us. I'm a widow. Without you.

21

Caffè Erica is a tiny place, at Number 19 on the street that leads up to the perched apartment. As I walk past with my shopping bags, I read that their spritzers are €2.50. I stop, thinking a bit of alcohol will do me good after so much emotion. I order a glass, and the owner – an older man who speaks a few words of French – brings it over to me with some olives. He sits down opposite me on a chair that's been cobbled back together several times already. There's no one in Caffè Erica. It's so small there's hardly room to stand inside. There's the owner's counter and a tiny door leading to a tiny toilet. Three tables outside. He asks me if I'm sad about something, straight out, just like that, are you sad about something, I think it must be written all over my face, in my eyes, even in the way I walk, how I get from one place to the next, my every move slowed by the molasses I'm toiling through, the cloying jam of this reality that keeps smacking me in the face, a reality without her, the truth of a life I'm going to have to spend separated from her.

One spritzer, two, three, four. I've lost count. My head's a bit wobbly, the old owner makes me laugh with his rudimentary French, no one's come to sit at his café terrace, I wonder whether it's like this every evening or maybe my sadness is driving people away. Or maybe it's you, my darling, sitting there with your waxy scalp, God, it's scary, such a gorgeous woman with such beautiful eyes, such green eyes, but no, not green, such beautiful eyes with their drooping lids and then a bald head, not a single hair. Come on, get up, let's go home. I walk through the encroaching darkness, my footsteps on the lengthening shadows on the pavement. I wonder what they'll be like in ten years' time, the winter evenings. I predict a house in the suburbs, not ugly but not pretty either, surrounded by houses that aren't ugly but aren't pretty either. The mist gives each street light an orange ruff, the tarmac in the streets looks like a long fish's spine, the few hurrying passersby gabble into their mobile phones with condensation coming out of their mouths. In the kitchen there's condensation on the windows, France Inter at full tilt on the radio, dinner to make for the kids, my daughter who's now huge slams doors and asks for a bit less noise, please, she's got homework to do. Grains of rice caramelize in the bargain-basement cooker bought in Belleville. Extravalue rice in extra-value soy sauce on their plates, which they take an eternity to finish, and it drives me up the wall, so I say, come on, you're driving me up the wall, hurry up a bit, and I immediately regret it. Satsumas for dessert, teeth and hands done, the radio beeping at 8:30, we get a move on, kisses and permission to read for five minutes. I knock on my eldest daughter's door, she's listening to crap music, she sighs, I don't keep trying. In the war-zone kitchen I automatically get on with the washing-up and listen to the world's woes on the radio. I think of the year Sarah died, an eternity ago, fifteen years ago. No one remembers that year now. The euphoria of our love is no longer even palpable. I can't access that life now. I've forgotten how to stroke her with the tips of my fingers, I've forgotten how to conjure the old memories of the young woman I was then. While I boil the water for my herbal tea, I wonder halfheartedly why I didn't have it in me to kill her, or rather why she stopped loving me.

22

Because yes, that was it, it was you who stopped loving me. You gave me that admission like a gift. And then what, what happened then? Then it was too difficult, the turmoil, the outburst, the despair. But we did love each other, and I remember that. I know how it goes. In that big house in the middle of nowhere, time spent getting the hang of each other. From the bed with its rough sheets I watch motes of dust glitter in a ray of sunlight and listen to her talking to the cat, do the washing-up, make a coffee. Mornings unfurl slowly as we work, she on her violin in the big room bathed in light, me on little prose poems in my friend's studio, peopled with paintbrushes, muted colors and exquisite sketches of birds. I'm constantly filled with emotion all through those days spent learning each other, those days spent letting our differences our similarities our discussions our fears our longings our squabbles our moods coexist and fully inhabit the place. I'm constantly filled with emotion by the clash between her concertos and my variety-show nonsense, her watermelon pips and my cantaloupe pips, her golden skin and my pale face. It feels so good spending hours working, each on our own floor in the house, knowing we'll soon bump into each other at the turn on the stairs, that our lips will meet on the landing, that soon the two of us will be in the same room again. It feels so good teasing out a point for hours, knowing we'll reach an agreement sooner or later. It's like in a film that doesn't exist but I'd have loved, if I'd seen it in the cinema. I want to learn them by heart, those days stolen from the summer and the precious moments scattered through them: the trip in the car with all the windows wound down and our hair in the wind, heading off to buy wine from the vineyard, suppers in the garden at the little sea-green table, her evening cigarette, which irritates me but which I relight when it goes out, laughing hysterically in the kitchen, the secrets exchanged, the childhoods described, and the looks from the butcher we go to three times and who thinks we're a couple of babes, oh yes, we can tell. There's a wonderful madness to watching her play, sitting on a stair in the big staircase, her eyes looking deep into mine, Bach sonatas that I know absolutely by heart because I've listened to them thousands of times on a record I was given for a birthday as a child. And there's the incredible experience of seeing her read something I can barely decipher, seeing her talk where I stammer, listen when I can only hear. She watches me step closer, watches with her green eyes with their drooping lids, my arms held wide for balance along the wire stretched out toward her. And with infinite tenderness she lets me say how I feel, talk about something I understand so little, with my awkward and sometimes inaccurate words. It's summer and – I remember this – I enter the world of music wrapped in her *humanity*. It's my sentimental education, and a sentimental education means where are you from and what's your name. Oh, my God, the reeling vertigo of love.

Trieste is an Italian city at the foot of the Dinaric Alps, on the Adriatic Sea, very close to the Italian– Slovenian border. For many years, before it was restored to Italy, it was the primary Mediterranean outlet for the

Holy Roman Empire and then the Austro-Hungarian Empire; this complex past and its position at the crossroads of Latin, Germanic and Slavic influences have forged Trieste's very distinctive culture and traditions. It has a population of 205,535. Its postal code is 34100. Its inhabitants are called Triestini. The perched apartment is on Via del Monte.

23

Waking again in the perched apartment, on the sofa bed that makes my back hurt. Waking again and listening to *The Trout* at full blast. Waking again to survey Trieste from the terrace overrun with seagulls who taunt me in my misery with their unfathomably spiteful laughter. Waking again thinking Sarah's here, in the apartment, thinking we're on holiday together, talking to her inside my head and then out loud. Waking again and knocking back grapefruit juice so I'm filled with acid to eat me from the inside, so that it all stops, especially that endless nagging question, what happened that night in Les Lilas, what happened. Waking again and again and again. The days go by.

Every day I live the same day. From the terrace I glance out over the city that throws itself into the sea, I run down the street full of happiness, then I head for the naval dockyard. I'd like to visit something else, there's so much to see in Trieste. But my footsteps inexorably lead me the same way. I've been doing it for several days, the same route, the same waiting, once there, in amongst the yellowing weeds, sitting on the little blue bench. I've been doing it for a week, maybe, I don't know, I've lost track. I don't have a calendar, or a watch. I'm a stowaway. When I'm tired of waiting I head back the other way, walking slowly and confidently, I go back up the hill through the city, I go to the Caffè Erica and have a spritzer, lots of spritzers, then I pop into Spar before it closes and I always buy a pack of gnocchi with spinach and some blueberry yogurts, which I eat on the terrace, watching the darkness creep over the city, seep over the sea.

Waking again and there's a storm outside, wild wind despite the extraordinary, unforgettable sunshine bouncing off a mirror and hitting me right in the eyes. Impossible sunshine. I don't think I've ever heard wind like it. It feels very strange in that perched apartment. Everything shudders, the walls, the windows, the door to the terrace. And there's a noise, a long drawn-out noise, a roaring, like an animal prowling, no, like a whole pack of animals prowling. I think I'm losing my way a bit in my thoughts. I even find myself thinking it's Sarah's mind roaring like this, Sarah come to take her revenge, Sarah come to ask forgiveness, Sarah come to tell me she still loves me.

I stay for hours, sitting on the little pale-blue bench. Every day I bring a postcard I've bought along the way and I write it in the white April sunshine. Or the May sunshine, I've lost track of what day it is, to be honest. I write to her, to Sarah. Address: rue de la Liberté – oh, the freedom of it! – in Les Lilas, back there, so far from here. I don't post them. I keep them, wedged into my bra. My bra supporting my faltering heart. At night I put the small wad on the bedside table next to the sofa bed. They watch over me. All these postcards I've addressed to you, my love. All these postcards where, at the end of the day, I always write the same words. Look after yourself. Get well soon.

Occasionally my day's itinerary alters slightly. I go and try on clothes in shops, I hang around in bookshops where I don't understand a single title. I vaguely remember my life before, my Parisian life, with my little girl, my parents, my friends, my job as a teacher. Sometimes I find myself crying like a child, racked with sobs on the sofa that I fold back up religiously every morning, as if it were the last, as if I'm about to leave Trieste and go back to France, to Paris, to my apartment, home. But Lisa made it clear they hardly ever come here, I know she won't be stopping off in Trieste for a good while yet. She told me to put the key in the letter box when I leave. I told her I'd be staying a few days before returning to Milan. I sometimes tell myself I'm going to put my things in my red backpack, zip-zip, I'll head to the station and buy a ticket to Milan, I'll board the train and, once there, get a cheap flight to Paris, take the high-speed Métro from the airport and pick my daughter up from school. But it's beyond my capabilities. My capabilities only just allow me to keep living the same identical days, enough grapefruit juice to destroy my stomach, to get me drunk on its sourness, the spiteful seagulls' insults, the walk to the little pale-blue bench in the naval dockyard with Sarah's ghost hanging on my coattails all the way, the picnic among the hangars, eating too-salty snacks, the walk back, the cheap booze with the old Italian man at Caffè Erica, the gnocchi with spinach and a blueberry yogurt when I've got the strength to make myself supper. And the horrendous nights, the terrifying nights, with the roaring that never stops, howling through all the gaps, the wild blowing of the wind that seems to want to insinuate itself right inside me, right to the very depths of me, an icy wind with macabre breath that knocks relentlessly at the window, gets under my dirty fingernails, under my skin.

24

I'm well aware that I'm losing my memory, that I don't know what day it is, that I've forgotten what happened that night. I sing myself nursery rhymes from my childhood, to get my memory to work. I recite the names of members of my family as if telling a rosary. I sing old French variety songs that I can still remember.

I tightrope-walk along the old rails at the naval dock-yard. One day I fall flat on my face, my arm crashes into a pile of scrap metal and a shard cuts me deeply. The sight of blood beading then running along my arm instantly reminds me of my daughter, I haven't thought of her for days. I remember that, blood in my daughter's mouth. Blood on her chin, blood on the ends of her fingers, blood on her tiny white teeth. Blood *evvywhere evvywhere*, she says. And – while I run through the snow with her on my shoulders, quick, quick, quick, while I concentrate on not slipping on the pavement, on getting to the pediatrician as quickly as possible, the pediatrician who's bound to be waiting for us already – my thoughts run wild. This century was ten years old when she was born, and I was twenty-two. For me, the color and smell of her blood will always be a direct line to her tiny body coming from inside me, to the earthy smell of her head that I don't remember but I'll never forget, to organic matter emerging from organic matter. That's me, organic matter. She's hoisted on my shoulders, spurting blood, and drops of it fall on my face between snowflakes, it goes white white red white. It's getting dark too, my freezing hands cling to her calves, I run even faster, I hear her laughing and I laugh too, relieved.

How many days have passed here when I haven't heard someone laugh?

25

One morning, the minute I wake up I launch myself at the cupboard where I remember burying my phone. I absolutely have to know for sure, to know whether or not she's still alive. I need to know if I can go home, if I can go back to a normal life. If the nightmare can stop, pause, come on, it's over. I open the cupboard, take out the pans and unearth my phone, I think about having to charge it and key in the code. I briefly picture the moment, all the anxious messages making the thing vibrate, sending it berserk with buzzing and beeping. I imagine my parents' voices on my voicemail, the voice of my daughter's father, of my former partner, maybe Sarah's voice, or the people who found her body, and I give up. I put the thing back into one of the two pans, put the other pan back on top of it, then change my mind, take the two pans out again, grab the phone, and the charger, run out onto the terrace and, without a glance at the evil seagulls, I fling the phone over the edge, throwing it as far as I can, I watch it cartwheel through the air for a moment and then smash onto one of the city's terracotta-colored roofs, down there, below me, between me and the sea.

It's suddenly urgent: I must swim in the sea. I don't know how long it is since I arrived here, I don't know how many times I've made this same trip from the perched apartment to the old naval dockyard, I don't know how many afternoons I've spent there sitting in the sun on the little pale-blue bench where I recite nursery rhymes from my childhood, but not once have I felt like going closer to the sea, even though its mauve presence has been a soothing influence since the start of my life in Trieste. It's because I know that it's there and it's alive – yes, at least *it* definitely is alive – that I can go to bed every evening. It's because I know it'll be there when I open the glazed door to the terrace that I can get out of bed every morning. It's because I know it'll always, always be there, no matter what happens, no matter what goes on, that I can keep on living. This particular day, the obsession mushrooms, I think about it all day. I'm restless, on my little pale-blue bench, I imagine what it'll be like, the smell of the sea, stepping into the water. I wonder whether I won't be able to get back out.

In the evening, almost too late really, I walk across the city barefoot, listening to the murmur of conversations from windows. I put my towel down on the pebbles. I inhale the slightly salty silt smell of the Adriatic. I watch birds quiver softly. The sea is pink, like the sky. It's hard to tell who's mirroring who in this whole arrangement. I step into the water, walking slowly. It's up to my waist when the smell of sludge overwhelms me and I stop trying to resist: I dive underwater and swim a long way, without coming up for air, letting myself glide. When I resurface many meters further out, I'm in the middle of all that pink. Small concentric circles form around me and drift away effortlessly. The sea is both smooth and caressed by waves, the sea is pink as if gilded with it, soft as a whisper, the sea is like the skin on a pan of milk boiling over. 8:47 in the evening, Sarah is dead and I'm naked in the pink water. 8:47, the sea is like the skin on the stomach of a woman who's had several children.

I remember this, I know how it goes. Her voice on the phone, when she tells me that's it, she hasn't got any hair left, none. She laughs, nearly, her voice is cheerful, the good-days voice, the loving voice, even though she insists on saying she doesn't love me anymore. She tells me the first treatment sessions have had the usual well-documented effects, the effects the doctors warned her about, she describes finding the odd hair on her pillow in the mornings, and then how it fell out in great hanks, the handfuls of it that came out in her hands when she tried to put her hair up before going onstage. I say nothing on the other end of the line, she couldn't care less, she keeps talking, she's not fussed about my silence, she tells me about choosing a wig, and then she describes that unbearable scene. I remember that, I remember my horror, my nausea and my hand clutching the phone, so tight, insanely tight, and my mouth too dry to get any words out when I want to tell her to stop, that all this is torturing me, that she's no right to keep me at arm's length and tell me she doesn't love me anymore while also telling me this stuff, describing this terrifying scene, I want to scream that she's a witch, that she's cruel, that she's got to leave me alone now, that I don't want to know any more. But her voice keeps going, unfazed, she laughs and says oh, it was funny, you know, it was so funny that we filmed the whole thing, I'll send you the video if you want, and I said no, no, no, inside my head, no I don't want, stop it, my love, I beg you, stop, leave me in peace, please. I remember how it goes, my heart slowing when she tells me that she did it with the other three members of the quartet, that they sat her on a chair and she closed her eyes, that they started with scissors, three pairs of scissors in their hands, they'd abandoned their musical instruments, those agile, agile hands that had become so clumsy, three pairs of scissors laying into her hair, snipping at random, and they laughed, it made them laugh mucking about like that, starting off cutting only one side, like some edgy girl from Berlin, and then the back and not the front, cutting to the chase, and taking photos at each stage, and then they moved on to the clippers, and they shaved her head, and they laughed, they filmed the scene and you can hear them laughing in the video, she closes her eyes and the three of them flit around, acting out God knows what macabre performance with their clumsy hands, their manic manitou laughter, while the clippers purr over Sarah's soon-to-be-smooth scalp. I remember how it goes, her face at the end of the video she sent, just like she promised, in among my messages, and I couldn't help watching it, I remember how it goes, her face already looking a bit yellow it seems to me, her eyes looking into the camera, her eyes with the drooping lids, the laughter on her lips, laughter I don't understand, that electrocutes my whole body, that I'd prefer never to have seen and never to have heard, the laughter that tipped me over the edge.

26

When I wake I hurt all over. I'm in a bit more pain every day. My body's often weighed down with longing for her body, for our two skins mingling together, for our fingers as deep as they will go inside each other, for our little hands intertwined. And the exhaustion that won't let up since she died. Sorry, since I left. I'll never sleep peacefully again. The exhaustion in my body and, at the same time, my body's extreme toughness, discovered by chance, it can walk for hours every day, can survive with almost nothing to eat and nothing to drink. If I go back, if I manage to go home, I must never forget the rediscovered childhood that I stumbled across here in Trieste. The little divided garden with its soft green trees serving as perches for masses of songbirds. The house on the street corner, opposite the electioneering posters, the corner house with one rust-colored façade and one in faded beige. Corrugated iron everywhere, wooden fencing demarcating the garden. Pebbles and the crushed flower petals on the pebbles. I'm going back in time. It's like being five years old again, it's as if I can sense the love my parents have for each other. Here in this rubbishy scrap of land lost on the far side of the world there's a taste of springtimes from my childhood. The infinite pleasure of having tea in the garden on the old white metal furniture, a round table and four chairs next to the three red-brick steps up to the garden, toward the loopy rambling vine that bears sour grapes. And the lunch parties, in our small garden in the Paris Basin, the lunch parties that I only now realize were parties, probably strawberries for dessert, in the bowl that looks like cut glass, pink cut glass, probably strawberries for dessert, with mint or orange blossom, and the juice running slightly on the white plates laid out on the white tablecloth. I wonder what it meant to people, being invited to Sunday lunch at my parents' house, what it meant to the guests. I wonder what those years were like for my parents, were they *the best years*. I walk through the streets of Trieste, always the same ones, as if there were only one possible itinerary in this city, and all I can think of is that bowl that seemed to be made of pink cut glass, that bowl my mother used for her strawberry salads at lunch parties when it was spring.

Why this reclaimed time here? Is that what I came looking for? It was completely irrational, upping sticks, leaving the child and my work, buying a plane ticket on a whim and accepting a lift to this place that means nothing to anyone. What if that was why? What if that was why I came to lose myself here, because it means nothing to anyone? I'm making this city my own, making this patch of land my own, making this life my own. Without you I'm still me, without you it's still springtime, without you it's still life beating like blood in a constricted artery. Is that really what I've done, run away just to spend hours at a time sitting on a little pale-blue bench? I'm going to find a word to describe the color of that bench, I really need to find a word to describe the color of that bench. It's not blue, no, not really blue. It's like your eyes, you know, my love, your eyes with their drooping lids, they're not green. Or if they are, it's an impossible green. The little pale-blue bench. I'm going to stay in Trieste and write on that bench for my whole life, my whole life writing things about Sarah. And about going back to my childhood. A packet of *taralli*, a pen. Writing, writing. I wear the same jeans and sweater every day, what's the point in putting on anything else? Birdsong in Trieste. Now there's a good book title. Birdsong in Trieste, the sound of hammering on corrugated iron, children's shouts filling the whole sky. Like anywhere else, and yet it's not really like anywhere else. How does this work exactly? Life, a user's manual. Writing or life. Oh, how I love the sun warming my thighs through my jeans and dazzling me, so I can't really look at the pages of the notebooks I write in so compulsively. A novel about those dead, mid-afternoon hours, in Trieste.

The owner of Caffè Erica and I have ended up getting to know each other. He doesn't say anything, greets me with a nod of his head, a nod of his smooth scalp, wipes his hands rather slowly on his unfailingly black shirt, turns around behind his tiny counter to make a spritzer, which he brings over, always whistling the same tune, a tune I've eventually come to recognize but not one that was familiar to me the first few times. The more days go by, the more wine he puts in my spritzers, the more days go by, the more food he gives me in passing, as if he knows I'm just eating *taralli* and, on special evenings – rarely – gnocchi with spinach. In the early days he brought me a few olives, and then one evening he put a saucer down in front of me with a little slice of bread with some pâté on it. I'm not very keen on pâté but I was touched and gobbled it down. The next day there was the bowl with the olives and the saucer with two slices of bread. Sometimes it almost amounts to sandwiches with Italian ham. One time, because I'd blurted out that I thought it was my birthday, he brought a tiny slice of cream cake, a cake produced from God knows where, revolting, and stuck in it was an old candle that had been used before. He'd sung the traditional tune under his breath as he set it down before me, with my spritzer − on the house for the occasion − and I cried. I went off to bed more drunk than ever that evening, I had trouble finding the door to the perched apartment's building, I didn't succeed in pressing the button to call the ancient lift so I went up on foot, somehow managing to climb the stairs, partly on all fours, with an urge to howl like a wolf at the moon, to howl out my pain, my loneliness, my madness.

A nightmare. I'm walking through the streets of Trieste, these streets I know well, these streets I tread every day. My streets. The paved walkway through the sweet-smelling branches, the American woman who sets herself up on the pavement to paint every morning, just as I'm passing, she arranges her easel, her pots of paint, her palette, and sits down, with her straw hat on her head, in a wicker chair to paint everything as she chats to passersby, and I do love to slow down to hear her delectable Louisiana accent talking Italian; the news-agent who always waves hello, and the little note I see in his window one morning saying he's going to shut up shop; the church further down, and the violets growing in the alleyway leading to it; the bicycle salesman with the beautiful salt-and-pepper beard, and his assistant who sort of comes on to me; the neighbors I recognize without really knowing them, the biker with the gorgeous eyes, the dark-haired mamma with her blond little girl, the couple I always meet in Spar, the granny with her little dog, the woman I imagine is a nursery-school teacher and her lover. A poster on a wall grabs my attention. It's a poster for a concert by Sarah's quartet, in Trieste. I look at the date, reeling, I read the name of the city and the name of the quartet three times, I stare at the four familiar faces, particularly hers, her dead woman's face. I don't understand why she agreed to be photographed looking so ill for the poster. I don't understand why she lets everyone see that she's going to die, that she's dead. Her bald head, her yellow tinge, and her beautiful long black concert dress. I keep walking on the route I take every day. I realize that the quartet coming here is the big event of the moment, there are posters everywhere. Her face peers at me from every street corner. When I get down near the sea I race over to a wall where there are three posters in a row, it's too much for me and I catch the corner of the first one and pull with all my strength, the paper resists and then tears and I'm left with a huge swathe of it in my hand, I hurl it on the ground and keep going, burrowing my fingers into the brick wall to tear off more and more of that paper colored with their smiles, I tear up their instruments, a great swathe of cello, a great swathe of the viola player's classy outfit, I tear and tear, battling doggedly with that wall, oblivious to the hunks of plaster under my fingernails, to the blood on the tips of my fingers, to the red smears that my raw skin is leaving on the recalcitrant paper, and to the crowd that's gathered around me. A man grabs me by the waist, yells at me in Italian, words I don't understand, words I don't want to understand, I must finish taking her face off the walls of Trieste, she has no right to be here, she mustn't come to this city, first of all because it's my city and also because she's dead, she doesn't exist anymore.

27

Some mornings I wake feeling a bit better, a bit less achy, almost in a good mood. I open the door to the terrace wide to air the apartment. I run myself a bath and rummage through the bathroom cupboards to find old lotions from the seventies that I put in the bathwater to make-believe. I steep myself in the warm water with its faded wafts of old perfumes and stay there a long time, my body suspended, with a semblance of peace at last. I bend my legs and drop my head under the water, my hair forming a curtain on the surface, I can't see the ceiling. My ears fill with water and, at last, I can't hear anything of the outside world. The only thing I can hear is the sound of my heart beating, I'm alone with myself. I take a deep breath before going to the bottom of the bathtub, and train myself to hold my breath a little longer every time, to reopen the curtain formed by my hair and take a lungful of air only at the last possible moment, when it really feels like my heart's giving out in the depths of my ears, that it's no longer so obstinate, that it's stopped being my ridiculously dependable metronome. I like feeling I'm on the brink of suffocation, feeling that this charming music box can suddenly shatter, that I need only make a little effort, stay underwater just a little bit longer, maybe a few seconds and it would be enough. What a class act that would be, to finish it all in the fusty vapors of the old man's ageless beauty products. A violet-scented death, what would you say to that, my love? Hey, I'm talking to you, you know. Bitch.

I mumble in Italian to the owner of Caffè Erica, telling him the howling I sometimes hear when I wake up is really weird, it frightens me, and I don't really believe in ghosts but I get the feeling a spirit's come back to haunt me, and I'm pretty sure I blush a bit as I say this. It takes him a while to understand, well, we usually don't talk, he just brings me the saucer with its bread and pâté and I just eat it, I put the money for the spritzer on the table and get up without a word, I feel him watching me walk away up the street to the perched apartment. He asks me to explain, what do I mean, howling, but I don't have enough vocabulary to describe the phenomenon so I start moaning, ah-ooooooo aaaaah-oooooo, he stares at me in astonishment, there's a moment's silence and then he bursts out laughing, he says but that, that's the bora, dear girl, and he explains, he says it all in Italian but I understand, it's like a miracle, è la bora, piccola, it's the bora, the wind that drives people mad.

I do some tidying in the kitchen. I'm putting up a front, the days have to trickle by somehow, and I'm sleeping less and less at night, I feel like setting out for the naval dockyard earlier and earlier. I can't seem to eat breakfast anymore, I feel so violently sick almost before I've opened my eyes, and I open my eyes a little earlier every morning. Sometimes it's still dark outside, I know I won't get back to sleep, I lie there on my back for several hours, gazing at the ceiling and listening to the wind howl, I know it's not the wind, it's you, Sarah, it's you howling outside the building, I know you've found me and you won't leave me alone. I'm frightened of going out on the terrace, even though I want to watch the sunrise over Trieste, I'd like to see the sun suddenly lighting up the sea as it emerges from indigo to put on its usual blue dress, its everyday dress, I'd like to count the various monuments I know, hear the first shutters open, look out over all that, even before the seagulls who hate me turn up. Be ahead of the birds, that's it, that's what I'd like. But your howling pins me to the mattress and I lie there like a corpse, I don't move so much as a toe, I mimic the way you lay, that night, in Les Lilas.

One morning when you haven't come, when the wind hasn't woken me at four in the morning, I decide to tidy the kitchen. There's not much to tidy, but I do some dusting with an old cloth, I put my few favorite utensils neatly back in their places and polish the sink. I come across the CD cover near the music system. And realize it's a double album. I've been listening to *The Trout* on loop ever since I got here, I automatically press the play button when I wake every morning and any evening when I don't get back too drunk, I've been listening to that lilting quintet twice a day for days and days, and I've never noticed there's another CD in the box. I put it in the music system. The first notes ring out. The sound of it instantly scorches me. I recognize the tune. It's a string quartet. I start shaking, my whole body's paralyzed. I manage to turn the case over, my eyes scan wildly through the lines of Italian for details of this second disc that I didn't see the first time. It's written. How did I manage not to see it when I found this disc that first day? It's written, in black and white, I'm listening to a Schubert string quartet.

28

I run downstairs, not bothering to wait for the old lift, I literally throw myself down the stairs and then down the sloping street, running to get away from those musical notes, to be done with them once and for all. I thunder into Caffè Erica, give the owner the same nod of the head that we give each other every evening, he doesn't seem surprised to see me so early in the day, at a time when I'm usually setting off on my pilgrimage to the little bench. I'm surprised, though, to see people on his café terrace, because there's never anyone here when I have my spritzers, people who look happy, eating their breakfast. I sit down, slightly put out because my usual place is taken by a young couple in sunglasses. The owner asks me *caffè*, Spritz, I say Spritz, I need a drink even if the city's only just waking up, I need a drink to forget those opening chords.

The quartet is called: *Death and the Maiden*.

It's later, much later, when it's nearly midday, and I know it is because people are coming out of shops for lunch, that I become aware of the catastrophe. My handbag's been stolen. There's nothing in it, just my wallet and a few pages written on the little pale-blue bench. The wad of postcards for Sarah is in my bra, the keys to the perched apartment in the pocket of my jeans. But I now don't have a wallet. No money, no bank card. I lose the plot. I push aside people sitting at the other tables, looking around for the thief, I call out to passersby in French, you haven't seen a handbag, have you, please, help me, I beg of you. I start screaming, making sounds I've never produced before, I think I won't be able to get home, I won't be able to hold my little girl in my arms, inhaling like an addict the sweet but salty smell of her neck, or see my parents again, reassure them, go back to work with my students. My bank card is the key to all that, the miraculous thing that means I could buy a plane ticket in a matter of minutes, buy a ticket, leave Trieste, come back to life. The owner of Caffè Erica says he'll come to the police station with me, he'll help me lodge a complaint, I mumble feebly no, it's not worth it, I can't face it, I can't face anything, but he insists, he says this has never happened to him before, and he knows me well now, he's grown fond of me. He says all this in a mixture of French and Italian, patting my head as he does, and I collapse in tears like a child into his heavy arms, against his black shirt on which he wipes his hands every evening before making my spritzer, I'm aware of his sweaty, old-man smell, I feel like telling him every-thing, from the beginning, starting with the sorcery of Sarah's green eyes.

I don't do anything, I stay there inert, the whole day, sitting on that terrace. He brings me spritzers, bread and pâté, every two hours he offers to close up the bar and come with me to lodge a complaint, I refuse with a shake of the head, he pats my shoulder, he brings tis-sues and I blow my nose on them noisily, I cry, making long wailing sounds, I cry so much it hurts, he brings me more spritzers, they go to my head, I talk to Sarah, stop looking at me like that for fuck's sake, don't you think I'm ashamed, I'm dying of shame, putting on this performance on the terrace of Caffè Erica, I'm dying of shame but I don't know what to do now, I don't know where to go now, the naval dockyard's too far, I'm too tired, the perched apartment is out of the ques-tion, there's *Death and the Maiden* there, oh, fine, go ahead, laugh if you want to, that's right, you can laugh, but you can listen to it without a shudder, can't you, you can listen to those four words, death and the maiden, because I can't, you see, I hear what they're saying and it makes me want to jump out of the win-dow, to climb over the balustrade on the terrace, to make the most magnificent leap of my life, it makes me want to fly off into Trieste skies and the restful sea all at the same time.

I eventually say no thank you to one last drink and decide to go back up to the perched apartment. The owner of Caffè Erica says that obviously everything he's served me today is on the house, and I can keep coming every evening just like before for my regular spritzer until I find a solution, I can pay him back later. He writes his phone number on the corner of a till receipt, when just the two of us are left, when he's totting up his day's takings, exactly as he does every day, and I watch him do it, exactly as I do every day, feeling completely destroyed. I turn the key gingerly in the lock, hoping the CD has stopped. I decide not to open out the sofa bed but to sleep in Lisa's grandfather's bed, in the kitsch pink bedroom, the bijou confection with its round window. I collapse onto the bed, surprised to feel my body sink into the pillowy mattress. I savor the comfort of suddenly being in a sort of nest. I feel enveloped by the huge bed, nestled in this quilted room, lost. I don't want to move. The walls pitch, the naïve subjects on the toile de Jouy fabric dance before my eyes, I want to be sick but my body's so comfortable I can't get back up, I close my eyes and try to breathe softly, to still the *dance macabre* of shepherds and shepherdesses on the walls and ceiling, to steady Sarah's voice, which I can hear inside my head asking who's the dead maiden, then, who is this girl who's died, is it you or is it me?

The bora is a katabatic wind produced by the weight of cold air dropping down from a high-altitude land-mass. It's a violent wind that blows swiftly over the city of Trieste toward the Gulf of Venice. It originates from a flow of cold air formed in the Slovenian highlands in winter, and it drops down from the coastal uplands, gathering speed as it progresses, with an average speed of 50–80 km/h and with gusts of up to 180 km/h in Trieste. The bora's name derives from Boreas, the Greek god who personified the north wind. It is called *borin* when it is light and mild, *boron* when it is a little stronger, *borazza* when it is very violent, *bora chiara* – clear bora – when it blows on a bright day, and *bora scura* – dark bora – if it blows when the sky is overcast. The French author Stendhal, who held a consular post in Trieste, wrote: "I call it a high wind when you spend the whole time holding down your hat and bora when you're frightened you'll break an arm." In 1830 the bora was so powerful that twenty fractured limbs were reported in Trieste. There are chains installed on street corners in various parts of the city so that pedestrians can turn these corners more easily, helping them hold on. And stay on their feet.

29

The next morning, in the bath with its eggshell tiling I massage every part of my body slowly, trying to encourage some life into my limbs, which feel dead, which might as well be dead. I recite the times tables, struggling when I get to three, I try La Fontaine's fables, clinging to things I know. I'm scaring myself. I wish I could remember what happened, that night in Les Lilas. I know we made love, that yes, but afterward. I've got the smell of blood following me everywhere again. It feels like the music system has started on its own and *Death and the Maiden* is reverberating all round the apartment. I can't even get out of the bath to check. I don't know what to do. Making a superhuman effort, I climb out of the violet-scented water, dry myself, put on my jeans and sweater, still the same ones, and go all the way down to the little pale-blue bench. I'm exhausted. I fall asleep straight-away, lying there on the bench, my last refuge, my hiding place in a hiding place, my escape within an escape.

The walk back is more grueling than ever. At the Spar shop I wait for a wave from the cashier who knows me well, and I wave in reply. I look around to see where the security cameras are. For the first time I'm not going to buy anything, I'm worried he'll suspect something, given I've been buying exactly the same things every couple of days for an eternity, or nearly. Grapefruit juice, gnocchi with spinach and blueberry yogurts. Apparently, some women have pregnancy food-cravings, I seem to have misery food-cravings. When I can get something down my throat at all, these are the only things I can eat. I wander round the aisles of the shop, I don't really know how to go about it. I glance around and slip the packet of gnocchi into the pocket of my moleskin coat. I leave and say goodbye in French, ashamed of myself, convinced he'll flush me out because of that, the change from my usual *arrivederci*. But he doesn't say anything, happy just to smile at me. I think the whole thing's disconcertingly easy and then, to calm myself, I tell myself I don't have a choice now, I don't have any money. Still, once I'm out on the street I do start running, I pass the Caffè Erica without stopping, so ashamed that it's eating away at my stomach, eating away at all of me.

The coming days are spent in the same way. I'm like an old woman, it takes me more than half a day to reach my little bench and once I'm there, I fall into a comatose sleep. It's almost dark when I head back up, I steal from Spar and no longer stop at the Caffè, I go back to the apartment, my body crippled with a generalized pain that I don't understand. I get feverish shakes, headaches so bad I want to hit my head on the wall. I try to write a bit, a few words every day, to keep my mind clear. But I can't remember anything, I can't work out what day it is, what month it is. My daughter's face is gradually fading from my mind. The only thing I see now are Sarah's breasts, her breasts which are so beautiful and so ill

they're going to kill her, her breasts which were the reason I killed her, and looking up higher than her breasts,
Sarah's eyes, her snake eyes, and her dead woman's profile wreathed in magnolias.

The String Quartet No. 14 in D minor, *Death and
the Maiden*, was written by Franz Schubert in March
1824. It was not published until after his death. Performances of the quartet last approximately forty minutes.
It comprises four movements: *allegro, andante con moto,
scherzo* and *presto*. The second movement, the *andante*,
is a series of five variations on a theme taken from
a *lied* composed for voice and piano in 1817. The
German words of this *lied* are from a poem by Matthias
Claudius.

THE MAIDEN
Pass by, ah, pass by!
Away, cruel Death!
I am still young; leave me, dear one
and do not touch me.

DEATH
Give me your hand, you lovely, tender creature.
I am your friend, and come not to chastise.
Be of good courage. I am not cruel;
you shall sleep softly in my arms.

I remember how it goes, her voice on the phone, when she was far away, in another country, in another city. How sweet it was knowing she existed; having *proof* of it. It's all I can think about now. The traces, the proof, the bodies. The embodied bodies. But most of all, most of all, anything *tangible*. Things you can touch while you still can. Tickle, caress, scratch; while you still can.

30

The shivers, the whole time, the moment I stir. So I've stopped moving, it's very simple, I've stopped moving. I skip the daily trip to the little pale-blue bench. I skip the spritzer at Caffè Erica, I skip Spar and the blueberry yogurts stolen while the cashier's not looking. I skip life. I'm cold, I'm really unbearably cold, and scalding-hot showers chafe my skin without really warming me. I keep hurting myself, bumping into things, cutting myself stupidly and my blood spurts onto the white wall, scratching myself with my own nails. I bruise myself. And fall over, smashing my face in. If only I could smash in the face of my lucky star, right now, just to see what it's like, or anyone's face, for that matter. Marseille's a bit far, a bit too far, even though I think about it every day, that giddy feeling confronted with all that sea and all that light, when I didn't yet know she was going to die.

I withdraw into the bedroom, the romantic old man's pink bedroom, the coquettish woman's bedroom when there probably never was a woman, the bedroom with the round window and the big gilt mirror. I'm in pain, I'm in so much pain, all over my body. Every move hurts.

I lie on the bed in the fetal position in the crook of the mattress, and wait. I don't have the strength to get up anymore, it's over. The hours go by, I can tell from the light sinking and brightening again. One night. I wet the bed. I don't have the strength to get to the toilet. My eyes are closed, my mouth is dry, so dry, and there's this taste of blood in my mouth. Two nights. I've stopped hearing the gusting bora, the crazy wind, the hubbub on the streets, Italian words, car tires screeching up the hill. All I hear now is the Schubert album, which still seems to be going round there, in the kitchen, again and again, tirelessly, as if a ghost presses replay the minute the quartet is over. All I hear now is the beating of my heart, to a rhythm I've never felt before, a breakneck tempo, *con fuoco*. It beats in my ears and my wrists, it beats in my snatch and deep in my throat. I'm reduced to this pulsing, my whole body beating time, a frantic cadence, a virtuoso performance. Three nights, I think. Maybe this day will eventually dawn. I'm so thirsty. Nothing hurts anymore now. I can't feel anything now. All I can see is red, behind my closed eyelids, red shapes flickering in time. Systole, diastole, systole, diastole, systole, diastole, ba-boom ba-boom ba-boom, just like that, faster and faster boo-bam boo-bam boo-bam faster and faster, faster and faster, faster and faster, like a tune getting lost in the shadows.

PAULINE DELABROY-ALLARD was born in 1988. *They Say Sarah* is her first novel.

ADRIANA HUNTER studied French and Drama at the University of London. She has translated more than eighty books, including Véronique Olmi's *Bakhita* and Hervé Le Tellier's *Eléctrico W*, winner of the French-American Foundation's 2013 Translation Prize in Fiction. She lives in Kent, England.

▣ OTHER PRESS

You might also enjoy these titles from our list:

NEVER ANYONE BUT YOU by Rupert Thomson

NAMED A BEST BOOK OF THE YEAR BY *THE GUARDIAN*, *THE OBSERVER*, AND *SYDNEY MORNING HERALD*

A literary tour de force that traces the real-life love affair of two extraordinary women, recreating the surrealist movement in Paris and the horrors of war.

"There's so much sheer moxie, prismatic identity, pleasure and danger in these lives...the scenes are tense, particular and embodied...wonderfully peculiar." —*New York Times Book Review*

THE PARTING GIFT by Evan Fallenberg

An erotic tale of jealousy, obsession, and revenge, and a shrewd exploration of the roles men assume, or are forced to assume.

"This breathless story...hits hard and never lets up. Terse, brusque, etched on one's inner thigh with an old serrated knife." —André Aciman, author of *Call Me by Your Name*

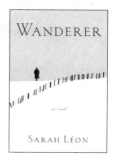

WANDERER by Sarah Léon

NAMED A BEST BOOK OF THE YEAR BY *THE ADVOCATE*

An exceptional debut novel that explores the stifled, unspoken feelings of a music teacher and his former student.

"The friendship of two men bound together by their all-consuming dedication to music is at the center of this novel." —*The New Yorker*

"An elegant and finely focused winter's tale. It starts out quietly dramatic and atmospheric but gradually builds and burns." —*Minneapolis Star Tribune*

Additionally recommended:

BESIDE MYSELF by Sasha Marianna Salzmann

A brilliant literary debut about belonging, family, and love, and the enigmatic nature of identity.

"A melancholic matryoshka doll of stories within stories spanning four generations of family, the novel is an exploration of the in-between." —*Playboy*

"[A] fascinating first novel . . . Salzmann's cool, disaffected narrative voice . . . is a wonder to behold." —*Kirkus Reviews*

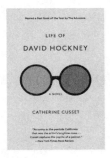

LIFE OF DAVID HOCKNEY by Catherine Cusset

With clear, vivid prose, this meticulously researched novel draws an intimate, moving portrait of the most famous living English painter.

"As sunny as the poolside California that was the artist's longtime muse . . . an affirming vision of a restless talent propelled by optimism and chance." —*New York Times Book Review*

"Cusset's book caught a lot of me. I could recognize myself." —David Hockney

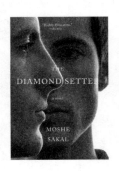

THE DIAMOND SETTER by Moshe Sakal

Inspired by true events, this best-selling Israeli novel traces a complex web of love triangles, homoerotic tensions, and family secrets across generations and borders.

"[An] essential read . . . [one] of 2018's biggest titles . . . a vital depiction of queer life in the Middle East." —*Entertainment Weekly*

"Richly evocative." —*Booklist*

OTHER PRESS   *www.otherpress.com*